A MEETING WITH MY MIND: POETICALLY SPEAKING

Terrell Wayne Hammond

Copyright © 2022 **Terrell Hammond** All rights reserved. To request permissions, contact the publisher at terrellhammond1@gmail.com

ISBN 979-8-218-04831-0

A Meeting With My Mind

A Meeting With My Mind

TABLE OF CONTENTS

INTRODUCTION	4
ABOUT THE AUTHOR	6
CHAPTER 1 A MEETING WITH MY MIND	8
CHAPTER 2 ANGER	31
CHAPTER 3 RACISM	51
CHAPTER 4 WAR	65
CHAPTER 5 HOPE	76
CHAPTER 6 JOY	86
CHAPTER 7 LOVE	91
CHAPTER 8 MELODIES OF LIFE AND LOVE	131
CHAPTER 9 PAIN	147
CHAPTER 10 POLITICALLY INCORRECT	160
CHAPTER 11 400 YEARS OF TEARS	179
CHAPTER 12 SUNSHINE AND RAIN	190
CHAPTER 13 THE POET	206
CHAPTER 14 FREESTYLE ALL IN A DAYS WORK	220
CHAPTER 15 MAY I RIP	242

A Meeting With My Mind

INTRODUCTION

Poetry: The art, theory, or structure of poems.

Poems: An arrangement of words written or spoken. Traditionally a rhythmical composition, sometimes rhymed, expressing experiences, ideas, or emotions in a style made more concentrated, imaginative, and powerful than that of ordinary speech or prose. Then there's the poet. A person who writes poems or verses displaying imaginative power and beauty of thought and language.

As a poet, I have been blessed with a unique talent to take some of my past and present experiences, along with the ups and downs of my everyday life and transform them into poetic form. My main objective when writing a poem is to try and uplift and inspire the readers of my poems through the wisdom bestowed upon me through God. Poetry is color blind and has no boundaries in the universe. The unique thing about poetry is anyone, young or old, Black, white, or any other color you may be classified in by society, can be a poet and inspire others with their poems, just as I have tried to do.

Like my first book, A Meeting with the Man Above: Poems to Inspire. A Meeting with My Mind: Poetically Thinking is a collection of poems I have written dealing with the everyday struggle it takes to make it in this cruel world. My first book was a collection of spiritual poems dedicated to the man above for strengthening me to make it this far despite all the obstacles that have been placed in front of me throughout my life. This book will deal with life, liberty, and the pursuit of happiness through my own words, exercising my freedom of speech. These poems will make you laugh; they will make you cry. They will make you happy and sad or even mad, but they will also take you inside my mind, the poet.

I am a product of the ghetto in Compton, California. A city that is world renown for all the wrong reasons. When I write a poem, I try to keep my mindset in Compton because I like to keep my poems as authentic as possible to give my readers a better perspective of me, the poet. When I write, I'm trying to touch my readers mentally and give them a more visual outlook to go with every poem I write. These poems were written while I was having a meeting with my mind. Meaning that whenever I write poetry, I am looking at everything mentally and meeting with my mind. I meet with my mind every day of my life, and the thing that is so great about meeting with my mind is I can do it anytime. Day or night, 365 days a year, anywhere I choose. My mind is always there for me to talk to, regardless of my mood.

As a poet, I try to write every poem and make every poem feel as real as can be so that you, the reader, can place yourself in my shoes. My main objective as a poet is to have the reader say things like, "I can relate to that." "Hey, that sounds like me." "I've been there before," or say, "That is true," and if I can get the readers of my poems to feel that way, I have done my job as a poet.

Poetry can be used as a relief for stress, grief, or suffering and can bring you up when you're feeling down. I've tried to cover many different topics in this book that many, you as the reader, will be able to relate to. Some topics are negative, some positive, some are sad, and some you may find funny. I've covered everything from life to death and everything in between. Some people sing to express themselves; others dance to express themselves; I write poetry to express myself. Therefore, as a poet, I suggest to all of my readers that you too find time to have a meeting with your mind because always remember, a mind is a terrible thing to waste. Think about it.

ABOUT THE AUTHOR

My name is Terrell Wayne Hammond. Born in Alexandria, Louisiana. I moved to Compton, California, in 1969 with my parents, who were searching for a better life for our family. I'm the third child out of a union that produced five children. I attended Ralph Waldo Emerson Elementary School and General Benjamin O. David Jr. High School in Compton, California. I went to Cerritos High School in Cerritos, California, and Cerritos Jr. College, where I received an associate's degree in Health, Recreation, and Physical Education. From there, I went on to Eastern Oregon State College in LaGrande, Oregon, where I studied Secondary Education and minored in Physical Education. I started writing poetry as a hobby in high school, thinking nothing of it other than something to do to pass the time in class. Still, I noticed I had a true gift for writing poetry.

I returned home from Oregon to start my own family, in which I am now a husband and proud father of five beautiful kids and one deceased at birth.

I took a break from writing for a few years, but around 1994-1995 I started writing again simply because times in my life were changing, and I began to look for a way out. In the 1980s and early 1990s, my city of Compton had taken a turn for the worst. Living from day to day, no matter what age, race, or religion you were, had become a task within itself. Murder, mayhem, drug use and abuse, gangs, unemployment, child abuse, teen pregnancy, gunfire, prostitution, city council corruption, and just plain disregard for human life were part of everyday life. As I grew older, I realized that the city of Compton was nothing more than an upper-class ghetto. Therefore, I am a product of the ghetto. So, around 1994 I decided to take the bad experiences of ghetto life and turn them into something positive.

I began to write poems about the good times and the bad, the happy times and the sad. I started sharing my poetry with family, friends, co-workers, strangers, and anyone who would take the time to read them.

In return, I was encouraged to pursue my writing to the next level. I would free-style write about any topic dealing with society's ups and downs or any topic from A-Z, always trying to keep my poems as real as possible so the reader could put themselves in my shoes and really feel what I'm saying.

The response was so great that I decided to reach for the stars with my writing, and I have really prospered from writing. I've won several awards. I had a column in a Christian newspaper. I traveled to Washington D.C. to attend a poetry convention and performed at some of the most well-known coffee houses and poetry venues in Los Angeles and Hollywood. I made guest appearances on two rap albums, published in several poetry anthologies and newspapers, and am now working on my spoken word album. My goal is to not be just another poet, but God-willing, another famous poet like Maya Angelou. On that note, I genuinely hope you enjoy my second book and use it to your advantage. Enough about me, let's get to the readings. See you in book three.

CHAPTER 1

A MEETING WITH MY MIND

A MEETING WITH MY MIND

I had a meeting with my mind, and this is what it said

Take care of me as long as you can; one day, we'll both be dead

Treat me right, don't do drugs, nah, we don't need to get high

Besides, drugs kill, and I don't know about you, but I'm not ready to die

I'm right here with you all the time to help you make it through the day

When times get rough, I'm by your side if you need to kneel and pray

Read and study, read and study, and fill me up with knowledge

One day I'll return the favor and help you make it through college

I've been here with you since day one, meaning the day that you were born

We've attended many funerals together; I was there to help you mourn

When something is wrong, I'm alerted if I feel you're having a bad thought

I try to tell you wrong from right because that's how I've been taught

We work together, hand in hand, trying to avoid a mental collision

When you need me, I'm always there to help you make the right decision

I'm not saying I'm always right; you know we've both made mistakes

As your mind, I'm here to correct them; I'll do whatever it takes

You're my boss, I work for you, I'll do whatever it is you say

When you make a decision, and I think it's right, that's how it will stay

A Meeting With My Mind

Sometimes you think an awful lot, and as your mind, I feel stressed out

I'm your friend to the end; isn't that what friends are all about

I notice you spend a lot of your spare time thinking about lots of money

What a coincidence, I think that way too, now ain't that just plain funny

We've shared good times in our life, and we've shared the bad ones too

What would I do? How could I make it if I didn't have you?

Remember the time you made a bad decision and it landed you in jail

I should have overruled your final decision that day; I admit I failed

Remember when you took that test in school, and your mind wasn't clear

You for me, me for you, together we have nothing to fear

The day you were very upset at yourself because you didn't have a job

I took control that day, I told you please don't go out and rob

Even though times have been rough together, we've made it this far

We both still have our sanity; just think how blessed we are

We didn't do drugs, shoot our veins, snort coke, or freebase

As your mind, I thank you for treating me right, remember

A mind is a terrible thing to waste

LIFE

Life is full of Sunshine

Life is full of Rain

Life is full of Joy

Life is full of Pain

Life is full of Hope

Life is full of Despair

Lie is full of Political Issues

Life is full of Danger Unaware

Life is full of Melodies and Song

Life is full of Sadness

Life is full of Peace

Life is full of Madness

Life is full of Anger

Life is full of Hate

Life is full of Love

Which we seem not to appreciate

WHY? WHY? WHY?

Heavenly Father, I'm holding on. I feel the end is coming soon

As I stare into the heavens high above, my view is being blocked by the full moon

I'm trying to make a connection with you; I want to see you face to face

It's terrible times going on down here, and the world is such a crazy place

I try to get in touch with you every day, and I do it because that's my choice

Hoping and praying on bended knees to one day hear your voice

Wanting you to lay your hands on me, wishing one day you and I can talk

Oh God, how I wish you and I could just take a long walk

I'd ask you first to forgive me for all the wrong I've done

I'd thank you for making the big sacrifice, giving us your only begotten son

I'd thank you for blessing me all the years of my life and always being by my side

Yea though I walk through the valley of death, you've been with me stride for stride

I want to tell you all the things that have been going on, but I'm sure you're well aware

Facing all my trials and tribulations with me, knowing that you were always there

Not once in my life have I ever doubted you; not once have you ever let me down

It's funny because sometimes I hear you talking even though you're never around

I want to ask you why, when times get hard, you let me suffer, and sometimes I even cry?

Why, after all these years, do you continue to bless me? Why? Please God, tell me why?

VOICES

It feels like the world is on my back, and the weight I can no longer bare

I want to give up then I hear a voice say, "Don't worry, I'll show you that I care

The pressure is building; I'm about to submit, I don't think I can take it

Then I hear this voice say, "Don't worry, together me and you will make it."

I push, and I shove, trying to throw it off; I push with all my might

Then again, I hear this voice saying, "Don't worry, everything will be alright."

Sometimes the pain is unbearable as the tears run down my face

Again, this voice tells me, "Don't worry" because one day I'll be in a better place

I feel weaker and weaker every day, so what am I to do

The voice tells me, "Don't worry, I'm here to strengthen you."

I try not to let it bother me, but that's hard to do sometimes

The voice says, "I'm watching over you because you are a child of mine."

"It has to get better someway, somehow," is what I keep telling myself

The voice tells me, "Keep the faith, trust 'Him' and no one else."

If I could just get this world off my back, who knows what I would do
This voice tells me, "The road may be rough, but I'm here to see you through."

I refuse to give up, so I continue to push each and every day
Then I hear this voice say, "Hold my hand son, and I'll lead the way."

I've heard this voice all my life, but when I look, it's nowhere to be found.
I hear this voice whisper, "I'm your Holy Spirit, and I'll always be around."

THROUGH HER EYES

If I look at this world through the eyes of my baby girl

I wonder what I'd see

Joy, love, and happiness

And how the world is really supposed to be!

SOMEWHERE

Somewhere on earth, a doctor spanks a newborn's little butt

Somewhere on earth, a casket is shut

Somewhere on earth, a kid learns to count to 5

Somewhere on earth, the ambulance drives fast to keep someone alive

Somewhere on earth, there's food being shared

Somewhere on earth, there's a crime scene being cleared

Somewhere on earth, someone lies on their deathbed

Somewhere on earth, an E.R. doctor shakes his head

Somewhere on earth, a problem child rages in a fit

Somewhere on earth, someone takes their own life to call it quits

Somewhere on earth, someone carries a big, beautiful smile on their face

Somewhere on earth, someone has died and are headed to a better place

THE GAME OF LIFE

God, this game of life is a hard one to win

Tell me, God, what is it about the color of my skin?

The odds are really against me, God; the stakes are really high

Sometimes I wonder would I be better off if I just die

Still, God, I try so hard to even the score

Sometimes, I must admit God, my life I wish to live no more

I pray for forgiveness every day for all the wrong I did

I wonder, was life this hard when I was a little kid

There's no place on earth to hide God and definitely nowhere to run

Sometimes I contemplate suicide at the hands of a gun

People say my skin is my sin, but God, tell me, how could that be?

There's not much to look forward to in this life; this is not the life for me.

If I should die tonight before I awake

Remember, in this lifetime, God, I took all I could take

Still, I admit I fought all my battles to the very end

Yet I will never understand why my skin color was a lifetime sin

Often, I screamed out for help, but no one heard my silent voice

You granted me with this skin color at birth, God; it was your choice

Therefore, I'm a winner, and victory I do claim

I wish this life on no one because It's been a cold, cold game.

SOMETIMES

Sometimes I'm up

Sometimes I'm down

Sometimes I smile

Sometimes I frown

Sometimes I'm happy

Sometimes I'm sad

Sometimes I'm joyful

Sometimes I'm mad

Sometimes I will

Sometimes I won't

Sometimes I do

Sometimes I don't

Sometimes I eat

Sometimes I drink

Sometimes I forget

Sometimes I think

Sometimes I go

Sometimes I stay

Sometimes I sin

Sometimes I pray

Sometimes I keep

Sometimes I share

A Meeting With My Mind

Sometimes I'm selfish

Sometimes I care

Sometimes I work

Sometimes I'm lazy

Sometimes I'm relaxed

Sometimes I'm crazy

Sometimes I'm wrong

Sometimes I'm right

Sometimes I will

Sometimes I might

Sometimes I win

Sometimes I lose

Sometimes I'm picked

Sometimes I choose

Sometimes I wonder

Sometimes I dream

Sometimes I'm humble

Sometimes I'm mean

Sometimes I creep

Sometimes I'm sneaky

Sometimes I wait

Sometimes I'm freaky

Sometimes I'm truthful

Sometimes I lie

A Meeting With My Mind

Sometimes I'm jolly

Sometimes I cry

Sometimes I'm slow

Sometimes I'm fast

Sometimes I'm first

Sometimes I'm last

Sometimes I stay still

Sometimes I'm on the go

Sometimes in my life

I just don't know…

CRIES OF LIFE

As I pick up my pen and begin to write

Holding in the tears of life so very tight

So very tight I'm gasping for air

Will someone please help me?! Does anyone really care?

I'm begging you society to lend me a helping hand.

I'm crying daily for a crutch to help this aching body stand

Many have offered their assistance which is nothing but a lie

I wonder would it help if I dropped to my knees and cry

I've come too far in this game of life for me to give up now; it's too late

Physically, my body Is deteriorating mentally; no one understands my mind state

As I search within to place the blame, life is like a sad song

It's instrumental with no lyrics, and the suffering tune has been playing too long

I keep hearing help is on the way, help I have yet to receive

My phone calls have gone unanswered, message I refuse to leave

As I struggle to reach life's finish line, wounded and broken-hearted

I refuse to give up, for I am representative for all the dearly departed

Or all those who have traveled the same path and endured life's pain

Something inside tells me there's still so much left in life to gain

For I realize life is nothing more than making preparations for death

Be grateful for the "life" you have and enjoy "life" 'til your very last breath

A Meeting With My Mind

GHETTO TRIP

Let's take a trip to the ghetto

A place where most of you have never been

A place where you can be betrayed

By the same person you think is your best friend

So, get out your tablets, take some notes

This ghetto ride has just begun

Many have challenged the ghetto

But very few have ever won

Yesterday I saw a little boy was dead

Get shot in the back of the head

The police came and covered him up

Which usually means the little boy was dead

There's no Cinderella, no Mother Goose

Don't even look for little Jack Horner

But you can buy some no-good rotten fruits

From the illegal immigrants on every other corner

The "ghetto" is known for its high crime rate

It's no big thing if you get mugged

And if you take a look to my right

That street right there sells all and any kind of drugs

To my left, that house with the bullet holes in it

A Meeting With My Mind

Belongs to police officer Booker

The gangbangers shot it up after they found him guilty

For shooting the neighborhood hooker

Straight ahead, you'll see a vacant building

That's where all the dope heads hide

Every now and then the police go in there

And find a victim of a suicide

Last week they found the body of a white girl

Who was here visiting from the valley

She'd been raped, sodomized, and strangled

And put in the dumpster in that alley

Now to my left, where all those trees are

Believe me or not, that used to be a beautiful neighborhood

And to my right is the indoor swap meet

Where they sell all the name-brand, imitation, fake goods

That yard to my left is where they raise pit bulls

You can tell by their vicious barks

Sometimes for fun, the gangbangers let them loose

To chase everybody out of the parks

To my right is the neighborhood shopping center

Every store in there is a victim of extortion

And to my left is an unlicensed medical center

Where all the neighborhood teenagers go to have their abortions

To my right, you see the community center

A Meeting With My Mind

It's the only place in the city where kids can go and have fun

And if you make a left on that street

You can buy brand new stolen handguns

They built this bridge we're riding on right now

To go over those train tracks

Because when people would get stopped by the trains

Every day 2 or 3 people would get carjacked

To my right is the neighborhood funeral home

Last week somebody stole a funeral car hearse

Can you believe they used it as a get-a-way car?

When they snatched the mayor's wife's purse

Down that street are the Criminal Courts building

The tallest building in the city

Judges hand down life sentences daily

And believe me, they show no pity

That bank to my left got robbed last week

They made everybody lie face down on the floor

They shot 2 bank tellers in the back of the head

And killed the first 2 police that came through the door

To my right is the cemetery you've been hearing all about

Where they were digging up and reselling graves

To my left is the street where they held that young girl

For 6 days as a sex slave

In the ghetto, they say it's mandatory

That every house has burglar bars

An on Sunday night, that main street right there

Is where all the thugged-out low-riders come hop their cars

They say in the ghetto, only the strong survive

But in the ghetto, they too take falls

Every time one is killed in a drive-by

They'll write his name and "R.I.P." on that wall

Now we're coming to the end of our tour

I hope you have learned something about the "ghetto" today

Oh yea, another important thing you should remember

That is, in the ghetto, you either play or you pay

You can play by the ghetto rules. You can even make up your own

Go down the wrong street, and "BANG!" you're gone

This tour is as real as it gets; it was not intended to scare you

I was just trying to give you some real and true facts

But by the looks on your faces, I can truly tell

You guys won't be coming back

to the ghetto!

FORGIVE ME GOD

Please, God, forgive me for all the wrong I did

I'm a father now, God, with a wife and 5 beautiful kids

They put all their trust in me, and I put all my trust in you

I've heard all about you, God, so what else was I supposed to do?

I heard you could move mountain God, I heard you could make it rain

I heard when I'm not feeling good, God, only you could ease my pain

Please, God, forgive me for some of your commandments I didn't abide

I know there's nowhere on earth I could run, nowhere I could hide

I'm trying to turn my life around and live by the "golden rule."

I want to be a good Christian God, no more Mr. Cool

You've given me more chances, God, than I think I truly deserve

You even gave me a book that explains your every word (the bible)

Please, God, forgive me. I'm trying to do my best

I've heard all the good talk about heaven, and one day, I'd like to be your guest.

I know that won't be possible if I don't have a clean heart

There were times I was about to give up on life, and you gave me a new start

When I was young, my mother told me something that I thought was very odd.

She said no matter what you do in this lifetime, you'll always be a child of God

A Meeting With My Mind

BABIES HAVING BABIES

Babies having babies at such an early age

The streets are the scene, not a Broadway stage

The little girl says she's pregnant, but she's only eleven

Just think, when you turn eighteen, your kid will already be seven

You dropped out of school because you said sex was more fun

Think about it, eleven years ago, your life had just begun

Now you're pregnant and think that's cool

Would I be wrong if I said you're a fool?

How you got pregnant, you don't remember; your mind was unclear

Why? You were high from smoking weed and drunk from drinking beer

You were fascinated by the motel room and excited that the sheets were silk

Your breast aren't fully developed you can't even provide breast milk

Your breasts aren't fully developed, you can't even provide proper childcare

You don't even have a menstrual cycle that's normal yet, and below no pubic hair

You stop going to school with a six-grade education

Now you have to depend on a welfare donation

The time has come when you have to tell your father and mother

The pain your parents will go through when they tell your sister and brother

That night he said he loved you, but you were only a kid

Now you can't find him to let him know what he really did

You're having cramps now and say the pain you cannot take

What you thought was a night of fun turned out to be a big mistake

Now you're four months pregnant, and your stomach is sticking out there

The guy is nowhere around to help ease the pain you can no longer bare

Still, you have your family who's willing to give you their support

You're upset because you can't find the father. Now you want to abort

You're six months pregnant now; the decision to give birth is up to you

You say abortion is murder, and that's something you really don't want to do

You made the decision to keep it because now you're already a mother

Hopefully, you will have your life together if you choose to have another

You lay there in tears and pain thinking about all those sleepless nights

In the delivery room, your mother is there to hold your hand and tell you it's going to be alright

You've been in labor for twelve hours, and suddenly at ten minutes after three

You gave birth to God's greatest creation, a newborn little baby

MY LIFE AS A SERMON

If I had to preach my life as a Sunday sermon

In essence, my life is a sermon I preach every day

It would be of great significance to those near me

And just as important to those far away

There's always someone critiquing my life daily

Or should I say, the sermon my life preach

So, I'm always cautious of the things I do

Being careful of what my life sermon will teach

I want my life sermon to tell a true story

I'll cut no corners or speak with no hesitation

Let my life sermon show all the adversity I've dealt with

And I won't omit all the trials and tribulations

I want my life story to represent me well

My life sermon would be the greatest story ever told

If I could translate my life sermon into book form

It would become the greatest book ever sold

If I had to preach my life as a Sunday sermon

There would be no need for tithes, gifts, offerings, or donations.

When I'm dead and gone, my life sermon will forever carry on

And the church congregation will give me a standing ovation

POPS, STILL MISSING YOU

Hey Pops, it's been 12 years, and the memories are still hard to let go

I'm trying hard to make it, and I love you; I just thought you should know

I have a kind heart like you, Pops; I'm trying to raise my family like you did

I have a wife and 4 kids now, Pops; I guess you can say I'm no longer a kid

I miss your guidance so much, Pops, and inside of me, there's it's still so much grief

Thank you for molding me right and helping me organize my beliefs

As a family, we're not doing good. I wish there was something you could do

When problems arise, I try to solve them as if I were you

I'm a big boy now, Pops; I'm behind the control panels of my life's flight

With you and God as my co-pilots, I know everything will be alright

CHAPTER 2

ANGER

"GUILTY BY ASSOCIATION" AS OF 1994

Yeah, "Uncle Sam," you run this world
This, I have to say

Please tell me where you are going to run
When it becomes judgment day?

Behind your badge, in your blue uniforms
Or underneath your hooded white sheets

Oh yea, the day is coming real soon
When you all will face defeat

Still, I'm gonna stick it out
Rain, shine, or stormy weather

I only wonder will I still be living
When times for Blacks do get better

They picked cotton for their masters
Our ancestors now rest in their graves

If you take a good look at today's society

A Meeting With My Mind

We're nothing but modern-day slaves

Years ago, a song was wrote
It started off "my country 'tis of thee."

Years have gone by, we have no liberty
And Blacks are still not free
I pledge allegiance to the flag
Is said in classrooms every day

If the Statue of Liberty was alive
Maybe she wouldn't even want it that way

Abraham Lincoln signed the emancipation
Which was supposed to make us equal

Hundreds of years have gone by
And as you can see, the proclamation has no sequel.

Since you've been in charge all these years
Tell me, what have you really done?

You forgot about the homeless and the Vietnam vets
But you let Oliver North sell the contra rebels' guns

A Meeting With My Mind

In the '60s, Malcolm and Martin
Our true Black leaders both came up dead

White people didn't want anybody around
Who was trying to help Blacks get ahead?

Let me just pause, take a deep breath
And let me just think back for a while

The Gulf War was led by a Black man
His name was General Colin Powell

In the '60s, the Black Panthers were formed
Whites referred to them as organized crime

But there were all white police departments in the south
Beating and hanging Black's all the time

Martin led marches; millions followed him. Why?
Who really knows?

He was only trying to bring us together as one
So together, we may congregate

A Meeting With My Mind

Yet, whites separated us by the color of our skin
Now that's what I call segregate

I wish I had the strength or the power
To turn back the hands on the clock

You say there's a Freedom Bell.
Yes, Black's stood on the auction blocks.

So, what have our leaders done for Blacks
As we keep wishing upon our lucky stars?

You've given us guns, drugs, and ammo
And, oh yeah, you've taken us to many wars

George Washington, our first U.S. President
Way back in the early days

Ran this country for years
Even though he, too, owned Black slaves.

There once was a president named Nixon
But for some reason, he just didn't fit

A Meeting With My Mind

Y'all voted him in as president.
Then y'all made him quit.

"I'm not a crook," is what he said long after his presidential debate
Oh, but later on, a crook he was, who masterminded the Watergate

President Clinton said he doesn't inhale.
But admits he took a few puffs.

Jeffrey Dahmer killed 17 Black men.
And walked into court without handcuffs.

President Clinton dodged the draft.
Because he wasn't all that thrilled

But he sent a young Black soldier from Compton
to Somalia, where he was killed

A Black lady named Shirley Chisholm ran for president
We all know she never stood a chance

Oh, but what a sight it would have been
Watching her do a victory dance

A Meeting With My Mind

I was born Black, and I'm going to stay Black
Until the day my life ends

All our life, we've been punished.
Simply for the color of our skin

Now sit back, relax, and kick off your shoes
And trip off these funky situations

A Korean lady shot Latasha in the back of the head
The judge gave her probation

During segregation Rosa Parks
Refused to go to the back of the bus

In 1992 Joey Buttafuoco had sex with a minor
And said it was out of lust

Amy Fisher shot Buttafuoco's wife.
And she didn't shed a tear.

Mike Tyson had sex with an adult
The judge gave him 6 years

A Meeting With My Mind

Ted Kennedy Jr. had a wild party
And the lady he was with yelled rape!

Oh, but white America didn't believe her
So, they called it a bad date

10 police cards chased Rodney King
Who was speeding down the street?

When they caught him, they formed a circle
And all 10 police watched this Black man get beat

The state acquitted the police.
But the feds say they violated his civil rights.

While two white police in Georgia
Beat a Black man to death with their flashlights

A former Black police officer did a sting on the Long Beach police
But his story didn't sell

They smashed his head through a glass plate window
Then hauled him off to jail

Then we have these two white boys in Florida
Even the jury knew they were liars

They kidnapped and beat a Black man
Then set his body on fire

Remember what happened in Bensonhurst?
Some whites were really thrilled.

A gang of whites chased a Black boy on the freeway
Where he was struck by cars and killed

Steve Howell, who is white, was suspended from baseball five times
Because he abused cocaine

Gary Pendleton, who is Black, threw a firecracker in the stands
And that season, he didn't play again

Marion Barry, ex-mayor of D.C.
Was caught smoking crack in an undercover sting

John Delorean got caught selling cocaine on tape
What happened to him? Not a damn thing

A Meeting With My Mind

The Menendez brothers blew their parents' heads off
Then said they were sexually abused

I know young Black men and women doing time in prison
Just for the drugs they used

A former mayor of Compton stole $5,000
To care for his ill son

Let me steal $5,000 from anywhere or for anything
And "thy will be done."

They say "let freedom ring," but if I recall
There's a crack in the Liberty Bell

Someway, somehow, I must admit
Society, you have really failed.

We drink the same water, breathe the same air
Yes, we still can't get along

Y'all have had all the presidents, vice presidents too
Tell me, am I right or wrong?

Society, you're not blind to all these known facts

Or should I say maybe you're just not seeing

Yo, Uncle Sam, forget treating us like "Blacks."

And just try treating us like human beings.

Q & A

Q

What can you do about something you can't do nothing about?

A

Save all your stupid questions, no matter the facts, just shut your damn mouth!

DAMNED

I'm damned if I do, damned if I don't
Damned if I will, damned if I won't
I'm damned if I quit, damned if I play
Damned if I leave, damned if I stay
Damned if I walk, damned if I ride
Damned if I surrender, damned if I hide
I'm damned if I win, damned if I lose
Damned if I'm picking, damned if I choose
I'm damned if I drink, damned I smoke
Damned if I'm rich, damned if I'm broke
I'm damned if I lie, damned if I cheat
Damned if I play fair, damned if I get beat
I'm damned if I sing, damned if I shout
Damned if I get in, damned if I'm left out
I'm damned if I'm up, damned if I'm down
Damned if I'm there, damned if I'm not even around
Damned if I give, damned if I take
Damned if I'm real, damned if I'm fake
I'm damned I laugh, damned if I cry
Damned if I live, damned if I die
I'm damned if I can't, damned if I can
Damn, the odds are against me

But I remain a strong Black man

LIFE IS A BITCH

They say "life is a bitch" then they say you die

Man, what a messed-up scenario, but why ask why?

The walls may come tumbling down; the road may come to an end

You may get stabbed in your back by a person you consider your best friend

Joined church to get some blessings; Baptist was my religion

Asking To forgive me, I've made some terrible decisions

I guess there were good times in my life offhand. There's none I can recall

I try to stand on my own two feet, but for some reason, I continue to fall

Hustled on the streets to make life better, got hooked on my own supply

Always dreamed of being a high roller one day before I die

Talked some girl into having an abortion; who am I to take an unborn life?

I was told you live by the sword you definitely die by the knife

Fathered 8 kids of my own by 6 different females

Didn't have time to raise none of them; spend many, many years in jail

Sometimes, I think back on my life, and it just makes me want to cry

If this is the life they call a "bitch" then I guess I'm ready to die

3 STRIKES, I'M OUT

25 years to life is the sentence for what I did wrong

3 strikes, I'm out, but in front of the judge, I stand strong

Trying to impress my lawyers, family, girlfriends, and peers

In my mind, I'm wondering how I will do all these years

Will I still have my reputation, or will it be lost with time

I wonder how many years will it take before I lost my mind

Would I be a model prisoner or my cellmate's sex slave?

As I leave the courtroom, I give everybody one last goodbye wave

Who'll be the new father to my 3 daughters and my handsome son?

I ask myself will God forgive me for all the wrong I've done

Time has run out in the free world; I guess this is the end of the game

I heard its hell in prison; I'm now a number with no name

They tell me survival of the fittest is what it's all about

25 years to life or 3 strikes

I guess you can say this time I really struck out

A Meeting With My Mind

SOCIETY'S CAGE

I'm mad as hell at society. My mind is in a rage.

Nah, this ain't no Hollywood light show; To hell with a Broadway stage

They say it's the land of the free; some call it the home of the brave

I'm free to roam from here to there, but I'm still society's slave

This world and the life I'm living is like that of a big fairytale

I'm free to roam but in solitary confinement, and society won't grant me any bail

So, call me Black, call me nigger, but I'm proud of who I am

Right now, at this point and time in my life, people, I just don't give a damn

I'm tired of being denied my equal rights or deprived of an equal opportunity

Yet, society keeps telling me to take pride in my fucked up ghetto community

Why should I care about a country or community that don't give a damn about me?

Oh yeah, and what do they mean when they sing that song, "Oh, say can you see"?

Nah, I can't see a goddamn thing, and society neither can you

Save all your patriotic bullshit; there's a problem with the red, white, and blue

I'm an endangered species running for my life. It's mankind that I fear

I scream and holler as loud as I can, but my cries seem to fall on deaf ears

Yeah, I want to go to the next chapter in life

But for some reason, I'm stuck on the same page

I just wish somebody would have told me when I was born

I'd spend my whole life trapped in society's cage

I'M MAD AS HELL

Yo, Society, check this out, man; I'm about tired of all your bullshit

I'm trying to live the so-called "American Way," and is this the thanks I get?

I'm obeying all your laws, your constitution, I even love thy fellow man

But, when I stumble and fall, and I sometimes do, tell me, where is my helping hand?

I honor my parents, respect the elders, and bend over backward for family and friends.

Then every time I let my guards down on you, Society, you slap me in my face again.

How much pain and suffering do you think I can take? Eventually, I'll have to fight back.

Please excuse my rebellious attitude, Society. Can you pass me that shotgun on the shelf?

Boom! Boom! Boom! Now Society, you tell me, how does that feel?

Give me the badge, the gun, the billy club, and let me kill at will

Let me kick in your door, search and seize your ass anytime I get ready

Let me be the judge, the jury, and 3 strike your ass for a crime even you call petty

Let me false imprison you, lie under oath, fix the police report, white-out key words

Let me deny you welfare, a car loan, let me cut your S.S.I. check

Let me see the fear in your eyes and watch you cry when the noose is around your neck

Let me repossess your home, increase your taxes, let me deprive you of Medi-Care

Let me place more burdens on your goddamn back than I know you can bear

Let me evict your ass because you're low on cash. Let me put your family on the streets

Let me make life as hard as possible for you and see if you can still make ends meet

Let me put you in solitary confinement; better yet, let me put your ass on death row

Let me put the handcuffs on your wrists so tight until you can't take no more

Let me lethally inject poison in your veins, nah! Let me pull the electric chair switch

Let me make your life as miserable as possible. Have you saying, "Damn, life is a bitch!"

Let me give you 40 acres, a broken-down mule, and a shovel, and sit back and watch you dig.

Man, I just want to put my foot in your ass, Society, but it's just a little too big.

I want to do you as you have done me; I want you to feel all my suffering and pain.

I want to make you all kind of promises Society, knowing you have nothing to gain

Yeah, Society, I know you're kicking back laughing at me, but realistically you're dying.

Face facts, look at the situation of the world. If you think I'm lying

I've been falsely accused and brutally abused by those who swore to protect and serve

See Society, I was born in the ghetto, lived in the slums, poverty is nothing new to me

Still, I hold my head high, with lots of pride, I am a man with great dignity

See Society, I know how you think now; it's better me than you

Society, you can't even look your own self in the eyes, let alone look at me face to face

You deprive me of my rights, dare me to fight, and totally abuse and humiliate my race

Blow after blow, down but never out I raise because that what I was taught to do

I stand tall through it all, not afraid to fall, and I know Society, God will deal with you.

Goddamn, I'm mad as hell!

CHAPTER THREE

RACISM

A Meeting With My Mind

BLACK

It's said when we die, we'll be reincarnated

Which means I'll be coming back

Be that the case, I have only one request

That is, I'd like to come back to Black

You see, Black is the color I am right now

And you see, I'd like to be that color again

But I'm really not the color Black you see

Yes, Society says that's the color of my skin

Therefore, I fetched a crayon box to check for myself

And according to the crayon, my skin color is closer to brown

Society, your main objective is to keep both colors down

Now, I accept the fact that, ok, yeah, I'm Black

But Society, your logic of thinking to me is wrong

I've researched my Back history, and my conclusion is

The color Black is very strong

For hundreds of years, the color has been abused

Oh, excuse me, I do mean the color, Black

For hundreds of years, with the help of God

The color Black just keeps on coming back

You see, the color Black is a beautiful shade within itself

Must I repeat the color Black is very, very strong?

You see, God blessed me with this color at my time of birth

Therefore, I'm more than sure there's nothing wrong

It's a shame how bad my people have been treated

Simply because we're Black

Society, you'll smile in our face, shake our hands

But when we turn around, cold stab us in our backs

Yet, we've overcome slavery, hatred, prejudice and forms of discrimination

And believe me, by being Black, we've had our fair share

That is of hard times, trials, and tribulations

So, when I die and believe I surely will

They say I'll be reincarnated, which means I'll be coming back

If that is truly the case, I have only one request

That is please, God, I'd like to come back, Black

40 ACRES AND A MULE

Yeah, I had my 40 acres and a mule

But somehow, I let them both get away

I held on tight; Lord knows I did

So, what else can I say?

They told me I was free now and slavery is a thing of the past

Society told me to hold up, boy! Don't you move so fast.

I was going to build me a house on my 40 acres, have kids, and a beautiful wife.

Oh, Jim Crow said that was too much like "living the good life."

A Meeting With My Mind

We just finished 200 years of slavery and hard labor too

Been beaten, shackled, hung from trees, what more can you do?

Raped my sister and mama, sold my bro and papa on the auction blocks

Threw my cousins overboard before the slave ships docked

Had me working the fields all day, not even earning a dime

Telling me to keep my head up cause soon it'll be freedom time

Word on the plantation is they're working on the freedom act

We're "human beings" with no rights, and society dares us to fight back

How did they expect me to harvest my 40 acres with a single mule?

All that tells me is they never heard of the "Golden Rules."

"Do unto others as you would have others do unto you."

It's a plain and simple statement, and it's really not that hard to do

Growing up, I was told, "All good things must come to an end."

I had my 40 acres and a mule taken away from me before my work ever began

A Meeting With My Mind

COLORBLIND

Close your eyes, pretend you're blind, pretend you cannot see

I have no idea what color you are, and you don't know the color of me

I know this is a touchy subject, but please let me state my case

Rarely do I write about this issue, but I'd like to talk about race

Not the "race" you do in competition but "race" as in the color of your skin

Remember, keep your eyes closed for a couple of minutes

Imagine you and me, best friends

Growing up, we did everything together; we were best of friends since kids

Our parents always talk about the good old days and all the bad things we did

They say we stuck together through hard times even though we could not see

Remember, I said we were best of friends, and that's how it's supposed to be

It's me and you against the world. We were down through thick and thin

Not once have you turned your back on me because of the color of my skin

Now, we're all grown up, and we still do things together

Remember, we're blind and best friends, and it's going to be that way forever

I've heard all about this "race" issue, but it's hard for me to understand

You see, I've been blind all my life, and I've been taught to love thy fellow man

A Meeting With My Mind

Now, how could I dislike you after all these years and all we've been through

Did you forget we're blind and could not see? Still, I have so much love for you

To me, everybody looks alike; I'm blind, so we all look the same

I greet everyone I meet with a handshake and call everyone by their name

I hear there's hatred going on around the world, and it all has to do with "race."

But, you see, I'm blind, so I don't worry about that; I just keep a smile on my face.

Remember, I said close your eyes, now open them and remember we were best friends?

Would you still feel the same way now that you see the different color of my skin?

Me, change on you for something so stupid? Come on, are you out of your mind?

See, my eyes are open, and thanks to you, I'll always and forever be colorblind.

FWEE AT LAST

Isa gun xkape frum dis hera plantayshun

Soone az et gits dawk

Isa gunna run az faw az isa kan

Den isa gonna waulk

Isa tyard pecking cotton all dey

Massa kallen me nigga

Isa tyrd ov ceein my peepel hangen frum dem twees

Ann dem ded bodeez flotin down da riva

Masa jumpen up ann down on mi nigga sistas

Ann dem got teaz n dem eyez

How culd masta b sew meen knot how butt whi

Wesa aint dun nuttin 2 dem

Butt wosh dem close ann scwub dem derti flowz

Isa den hade enu ov dis hera

Sew nowa isa gotta go

Me donnt kno where me go n

Butt itz gone be wheel faw

Isa kaint weed ow whrite

Sew isa gun follow da bwitest staw

Isa gone go tale sumbodi

Whot bee gowin onn bak dehre

Ha wee work frum sunwise to sunsit

A Meeting With My Mind

Ann massa doent evin kare

Isa gone show sumbodi deez numbas dey bwanded on mi back

Ohh chit what dis hera

Luok like sum whalwhode twacks

Now isa wememba ah stowi on da plantashun I wuz tole

Both dis ladi nahyme hawwiet tubbmen

Wonnin dis ting kaled da undagwond walwold

Now isa gonna follow dees here twacks ann chaze da wissin sunn

Ann isa eint gone stop chazzindem

Til isa finne me su fweedum

A Meeting With My Mind

IF I WAS BLIND

If I was blind and could not see
There would be no prejudice inside of me

I would treat everyone the same
I'd call every human being by their name.

I would learn to appreciate life a little more.
I couldn't see the difference between rich and poor.

I'd probably have a hard time finding a job
I know for a fact I could never go out and rob

I wouldn't be able to see all the big fancy cars
I couldn't look up at night and count the bright stars.

I couldn't see all the violence and hate
I could never drive my girlfriend out on a date

I couldn't go shopping and spend lots of money.
I can't see, but I sure can hear when something is funny.

I wouldn't know the meaning of a bright sun shining day

A Meeting With My Mind

I could only see darkness seeing life my way

I wouldn't want to be denied mankind's "love."
I could only imagine the beauty of a snow-white dove.

So, I wonder if I was blind and could not see
Would this world they call society care about me?

ISA FWEE

Isa owne my whay 2 fweedum tukmeeza myte, myte loung tyme
Isa dun say e meself sum munny ah hole quatta, 2 nikels anna dhyme
Isa retyerd now dun spint iftee yeres owne massa plantatshun
Ole massa ann his old wife putt me own dis here ole twain
Ann tole me 2 takes meself a baycation
Now massa sayzz isa ainte wurff nutin now
Massa tole me day dun gott day munnyies worrf
Y massa tole me dey payed a hole 25 dolla's 4 me
At my tyme uf berf
Massa tole me my mommie had big bwessesses
Nappi hare ann big lipps
Say she scweemed ann begged 4 dem knot 2 take me
Ti massa poppeded her with dat wipp
Sew kan 1 uf u yungins tale me whot It like b n fwee

A Meeting With My Mind

Kuz Isa frum da ole skoo Isa memba ov slabery

Hay mr kunducta put owne dim ole bwakes

I meen slo dis ole twain downe

Kuz Isa wonts 2 git off write cheer

Ann placse my feet own solid growne

Weeza n da 2000 now ann slabery izz a ting ov da pass

Ainte no mo gib up dat seet 2 no wite man

Ainte no mo go n lass

Well, iheerd day dun wung da fweedum bell

Now Isa gone scweem ann shout

No mo pickin kotten 4 massa jones

No mo hangins back dehre in da souf

Now Isa gone steels ma a horse ann ride like paul reveer

Isa gone tell dem da nigga's r cuming da nigga's r cuming

Put sum ole fear n dem ole massa's hart

Make dem ole boyz start runnen

No mo sweit an tearzz wonnin down my face

No mo wurkin round da clocc

Isa gone takez me za hamma

Imo tar down dem ole ockshun bloccs

Isa gone sabe 1 fo me ann stan own it

Isa gone let da storee b tole

I'mo yale out 2 ole hawieet tubmen

Shutt downed at ole undagwound whalerode

A Meeting With My Mind

No mo salen own dem ole slabe shippzz

Got niggas cwamed up on da bottom deck

Isa gone tale dem ole kkk boyzz

Put dem nooses round day owne necks

No mo bwanden me own my back wit dat hot iren

Like isa sum kattle n da feel

Kuz god gone punish dem ole redd necks

Da 1's dat killed lil Emmit Till

No mo kerrpin n my shack steelin my nigga sist'a

No mo rapin dem n da middal ov da nite

Y massa mus ainteherd da guud newz

Y day dun gave us sum wites

No mo kallin me mandingo

No mo haven me studd da massa'a stanky wife

Isa aw fwee nigga boy now

Isa gone stawt me a neew life

Isa gone stawt me a neew genawation

Isa gone make me sum butyful black little kidzz

Ann let God punish dem ole slabe massa's

4 whut dem ole boyz done did

Sew tale chickin George, kunta kent'e

Ann pleezze don't 4get aint kizzzy

Letz go scweeeeeeeeme ann shoout an yell hahlaylcwyah

B cuzz God don set us a fwee

THEY CALL ME NIGGER

They call me nigger because my skin is black

They told my ancestors to shut up and don't talk back

They call me nigger and say I'm dumb

When all odds are against me, I'm still #1

They call me nigger because I have nappy hair

Is that really a reason to treat me unfair?

They call me nigger and say I'll always fail.

That really strengthens me more and makes me prevail

They call me nigger because they think it's funny

But I love myself like a bee loves honey

They call me nigger and make me lay face down on the ground

They cuff me, kick me, beat me, but they still can't keep me down

They call me nigger and tell me I'll never make it

The noose gets tight sometimes, but I always seem to break it

They call me nigger and criticize everything I do

Yes, they wonder why I don't have much respect for the red, white, and blue.

They call me nigger and take away my inevitable rights

I feel no remorse as I continue to struggle and fight

They call me nigger and consider my skin color second class

Hundreds of years later, they still don't realize slavery is a thing of the past

They call me nigger and label me a felon; now I can't even vote

A Meeting With My Mind

One can only imagine the pain a slave must have felt hanging by their throat

They call me nigger, deny me education and financial aid

I'm willing to learn all that I can; Like everybody else, I want to get paid

They call me nigger, coon ass; I have a name, but they continue to call me "boy."

God gave me this life, too, so "they'll" have to understand

This is my life to enjoy

CHAPTER FOUR
WAR

ONCE I LIVE AGAIN

I promise I'll live my life different once I live again

My soul is gone, I have no remorse

Still, society I'm begging you

Will you please forgive me for my sins?

I've left this world the same way I came here

That is, all by myself

To all my family and friends, I'm gone now

Throw away all those trophies on the shelf

I totally threw this life away

I'm probably going to hell

I don't want sympathy from nobody

I must admit society I failed

I'm living now in spirit

This lifetime I live no more

Those who feared me need not worry

I'll no longer be knocking at your door

I'm on my way somewhere

Hopefully I'll meet new friends

But, I promise you society I'll live my life different

ONCE I LIVE AGAIN....

A Meeting With My Mind

4TH OF U-LIE

Fireworks bright and beautiful light up the night sky

It's Independence Day; I mean, it's the 4th of Ju-lie

Independence; free from the control, influence, and support

Or help from others

For some reason, I just don't agree with that; my sisters and brothers

Especially the part that says free from "control."

Let's see, we have insurance control, tax control, welfare control, gun control, rent control, birth control, and flood control, last I was told.

Then there's the part that says free from the support or help from others

So, what's that telling all of our single-parent mothers?

That regardless of your struggle or the tears that continue to fall from your eyes.

We have 1 day a year to celebrate our independence, that's the 4th of Ju-lie.

My birthday is in November, but I don't use it to celebrate

I'm still waiting for my independence from society's wrought iron gates

Independence Day, a holiday honoring the signing of the Declaration of Independence on the 4th of Ju-lie

I spend the other 364 days of the year chasing my dreams as they dash across the skies

Independence Day, don't get me wrong, I celebrate like hell on the 4th of Ju-lie

Not because of my independence, but um, um, um, damn, I don't even know why

BLACK ON BLACK

Black on Black crime, now that's just plain dumb

When in reality, it should be one for all and all for one

Now someone help me understand; how much sense does that make?

What is your reward for a brother's life you choose to take?

Take a look back at slavery. Our ancestors all suffered the same

But you choose to pick another Black brother to inflict great bodily pain

History shows 200 hundred years ago, all of our ancestors were slaves

So, why do you choose to kill another brother and send him to an early grave

History also shows our ancestors came over here shackled on overcrowded boats

When they disobeyed their master's orders, they were usually hung by their throats

Black on Black crime makes no sense because we're all from the same race

For Blacks to kill Blacks the way we do today is just a damn disgrace

If I remember, one of God's commandments says, "thou shall not kill."

Yet, you use a gun just for fun and kill one another to get a thrill

Think of the struggle our ancestors went through for us to get this far

You kill your brother who had dreams of one day becoming a movie star

Blacks killing Blacks, why? Because this rag is red and yours is blue?

Our blood is all the same color, brother, when the coroner goes inside of you.

Statistics show Black on Black crime is at an all-time high

Pass by any funeral home on any given day and hear our brothers and sisters cry

Black on Black crime, please, brothers, think about it. It's happening every day

Believe me, brothers and sisters, there is a better way

So, wake up, brothers. The clock is ticking. Time is passing us by

What's more important, the will to live, or should I say the will to die?

A Meeting With My Mind

GOD BLESS OUR TROOPS

Sitting out one cozy night, gazing up at the stars

It's 12:01 am, and we're about to start a war

It's 1991; somebody, please tell me the government is lying

Let's think about all the innocent loved ones that will be dying

In August 1990, you know Iraq invaded Kuwait

The President said January 15th was the deadline date

Think of all the tears and sorrow war will bring

And to declare it on the birthday of the late Dr. Martin Luther King

To kill thousands of innocent people for such an unworthy cause

Please, Mr. President, Congress and the senate take time out and pause

Just take time out of your busy schedules and think about what you're doing

Just think about all the loving families that this war will be ruining

It's bad enough that people are dying from starvation, leukemia, aids, and even cancer

I'm begging you, Mr. President, work on another solution because war is not the answer

It's January 16th now as the world watches the hours pass by

We all wonder what our troops are thinking as they gaze up in the sky

With tanks, big guns, fighter planes, and very big battleships

I pray that none of our troops have made a one-way trip

They're mothers, fathers, sisters, and brothers

They're uncles, aunts, friends, and many others

Who will be putting their lives on the battlefields?

A Meeting With My Mind

We all know when this war starts, it's kill or be killed

You guys served, fought, and died for "our country tis of thee."

As our country engaged in enemy warfare

You guys were instrumental in helping keep this country free.

Please Mr. President, reach for a better solution for this terrible situation

There has to be a better solution just have a little more patience

Both countries say they are ready to fight with big guns in their hands

To protect and serve and fight to the end for Saudi Arabia's rich oil filled land

Please Mr. President let's reach some peaceful agreement so that none of our troops get killed

And all of the world's prayers somehow be fulfilled

It's been done before and I'm sure it can be done again

A war that ended before it ever began

Just think Mr. President a war that ended with no shots fired and no lives lost

Victory for both countries at a very, very, very, low cost

All our troops coming home to their families full of joy and happiness again

That's how it was before they left and before all this madness began

Please Mr. President bring them back home to their loved ones that's where they belong

Do it before the "war" starts because we all know going to "war" will be wrong

So as we sit and wait for the war to start "troops" we all send our LOVE

And hope our prayers are answered from the Heavenly Father high above

After all these years, you guys were never given your "just reward."

So personally, I feel like this is something I must do

So, on behalf of me and the thousands of other Nego Americans

We extend our right hand to say, "thank you."

A Meeting With My Mind

WALKING IN DISGUISE

This world is being run by people who think they know it all

The real truth is their thinking is very small

The earth is being destroyed with all their modern education

Still, they want us to think they've reached their expectations

Really, to be honest, they're not as smart as they may believe

Money, computers, and ignorance have their poor minds deceived

Yeah, they can build the big jumbo planes to travel across the skies

Doctors can transplant the human heart and even the human eye

NASA can build the space shuttles to explore the heavens above

But they have no skills whatsoever when it comes to building "love."

Our so-called leaders stand on the podiums and tell us exactly how they feel.

Then make us as citizens pay taxes for their big weapons to kill

We as citizens can't own guns, but our leaders can own bombs

A man-made device they build to kill in greater sums

If our so-called leaders don't change their destructive ways

With millions of innocent lives is the price we'll all have to pay

I'm sure there are others who feel this way, and to me, we are truly civilized

This, to us, leaves all our so-called leaders merely walking in disguise

NO TO WAR

What's wrong with this world we live in today?

It's 2003, and we're headed to war

With all the other problems we already have

War is the last thing we need by far

I mean, can't we all just get along for once?

Let's work together to make this world a better place

Let's make peace and love universal

Regardless of color, creed, or race

Can we love thy fellowman for a change?

No matter what country he or she is from

Because in the eyes of the Creator, we're all the same

He created us all equal as one

Can we lend a helping hand to our fellow countrymen?

If he or she should fall

And hopefully, they'll do the same for us

If our country should ever call

Let's attack world hunger and world starvation

From every corner of the world

Let's work together to make sure no one goes hungry

That includes every man, woman, boy, and girl

I mean, we drink the same water, breathe the same air

Believe it or not, we still can't get along

I say it again LOVE and PEACE is the only answer

And WAR would be so very, very wrong

CHAPTER FIVE
HOPE

STOP, LOOK, AND LISTEN

When friends try to hold you down, believe me, as they often will
When the brakes seem to have gone out when you're going downhill
When your money is running low, and your bills are extremely high
When you laugh at everything knowing you'd rather cry
When you're tired of living in the fast lane, slow down a little bit
Stop, look, and listen, but please just don't quit
You've worked from sunrise to sunset just to get this far
Why stop now? Keep going, make your destination the brightest star
Take a big hammer and knock down anything that gets in your way
You finished yesterday; plan for tomorrow as you try to conquer today
To reach your goals in life, you must slow down a little bit
Stop, look, and listen, but please just don't quit
Strive to do your best in life. That's all you can possibly do
Look for true friends that won't be easy; true friends are far and few
Never surrender, even though life is not always fair
But why quit now? Continue to run; believe me, you're almost there
Pace yourself for the long run; slow down just a little bit
Stop, look, and listen, but please just don't quit
Tell yourself over and over again, "I will not fail."
With self-preservation and determination, your ship will continue to sail
Regardless of the weather, I know the waters will be rough
For I am a child of God, so I know I'm built tough

When life seems to rush you, slow down a little bit

I see the finish line right up ahead. Thank God I didn't quit

JUST WISHING

I watched the sunrise this morning

I watched the darkness turn to light

I thanked God for another breath of life

Hoping today everything will be alright

Many things will happen in the world today

Some good things and, of course, some bad

Hopefully, for me, everything good will happen

Because the bad days, enough of them I've had

I wish the best for my family

Wishing we all live to see another day

I wish the same thing for the entire world

If only I had things my way

I wish for peace throughout the world

From sea to shining sea

I wish for love and unity throughout the community

Oh God, how I wish this is how the world could be

If I could, I'd stop the wars that are going on

With the stroke of a pen, I'd bring all the wars to an end

I wish I could line up all the soldiers in every country

Have them all shake hands and be friends

Imagine a day with no one dying

Be it murder, sickness, or natural cause

A Meeting With My Mind

I wish we could all live just one day in this lifetime

Where everyone would respect and obey man's laws

What happened to the saying "love thy neighbor"?

My parents taught me to always love thy fellow man

Regardless of race, creed, or the color of a person's skin

If I should fall in your presence, please lend me a helping hand

Close your eyes for just a minute

Act as though you could not see

Make a wish for the good of the world today

I wonder will your wish include me

ONCE I LIVE AGAIN

I promise I'll live my life different once I live again

My soul is gone; I have no remorse; still, will you forgive me for all my sins?

I've left this world the same way I came, and that is all by myself

Tell my parents I'm gone now, throw away all those trophies on the shelf

I totally threw this life away; I'm probably going to hell

I don't want no sympathy from nobody; I must admit I failed

I'm living now in spirit. This lifetime I live no more

Those who feared, don't worry; I won't be knocking on your door

I'm on my way "somewhere" hopefully, I'll meet new friends

But I promise I'll live my life different once I live again

A Meeting With My Mind

BY MY NAME ALONE

I want to be something in this lifetime

God, please make something out of me

I just want to be known by my name alone

I just want to be all I can be

I don't want to be a millionaire

What the hell would I do with a million bucks?

You see, I'm a product of the ghetto

And most of my life, I've been down on my luck

I could never be a big-time movie star

I have very few reasons to smile

Still, I've been dreaming of making it big

Every since I was a little child

I don't want to be a doctor or lawyer

Those people spend too many hours away from home

Besides, I can hardly help my own self

And I have enough problems of my own

What if I was a high-priced sports player?

Nah, because basketball is not my sport

But I'd probably look good in a long black robe

Being a Black judge sitting on the Supreme Court

I don't want to be a police office

I'm really not good at fighting crime

A Meeting With My Mind

How would I look arresting someone for panhandling?

Or should I say begging for nickels and dimes?

You see, I really want to be something in this lifetime

God blessed me with a gift, and I have proof to show it

I just want to be known by my name alone

Terrell Wayne Hammond, the "poet."

A Meeting With My Mind

WILL THERE EVER BE

It's 2006, and can you believe we're still being separated by race

This world we live in today, I must admit, is such a crazy place

Race as in color, or should I say, the color of our skin

Who knew at their time of birth your skin color would be a sin?

Some people are blind to the fact, or maybe they're just not seeing

God created us all equal as one, that being human beings

We breathe the same air, drink the same, and we still can't get along

I don't think that was the master's plan; somewhere in society, we went wrong

You see, God blessed us with our skin color, be it Black, white, brown, or blue

So, what reason do you have to hate me, and what reason do I have to hate you?

Why can't we love each other for who we are, disregard the color of our skin

Race should not play a part at all when it comes to choosing a friend

We should all be able to love one another. We should all lend a helping hand

I'm sure when God created the heavens and earth, this was his plans

Close your eyes for a moment and pretend you could not see

Now, race has no color, it's invisible, and I think that's how it should be

We should all be judged for who we are, and race should play no part

Hundreds of years have passed us by, but it's still not too late to start

Will we as a human race ever wake up? Will this race thing ever cease?

Will this world ever be filled with love, harmony, and most of all, peace?

CHAPTER SIX

JOY

SMILE FOR ME

I'd like to write about a prized possession we all possess

It's known throughout the entire word

When I say "all," I do mean "all."

"All" meaning every single man, woman, boy, and girl

It's been around since the beginning of time

We all inherit it at our time of birth

No one could ever take it from you

And its power can match any amount of dollars' worth

Some say it's part of the dairy product family

It's usually used in the same category as cheese

Countries use it as a sign of victory

Some countries use it to greet their enemies

I know right now you're a little confused

But all comparisons you read will be so very, very true

I use this prized possession at daily myself

And I bet a million dollars so do you

You may use this prize possession at nighttime

You may use it at any time of the day

No matter how you use it, it means the same

When you find out, you'll believe every word I say

This prized possession is so powerful

It's mightier than any medieval sword

A Meeting With My Mind

You see, people use it when they're by themselves

Or in groups but on the same accord

It's universal and understood by all

Regardless of age, sex, or race

Two countries once used this prized possession

When they met each other up in space

This prize possession is used daily on television

This prized possession can be found from school to school

I really can't understand one thing about it

Why was it excluded from man's "Golden Rule"?

Some use this prized possession for personal gain

Some use it from the bottom of their heart

Like I said in the beginning, some use it as a form of a greeting

Some people use it when it's time to depart

By now, I'm sure you're really confused by all this

You're probably wondering what this prized possession could be

I just wanted you to use your mind for a minute

And as a poet, I ask that you don't get upset with me

I know as a reader, you may think this is wrong

But as a poet, I just wanted you to really think for a while

This big, prized possession we all possess

It is known simply as a little smile

Smile for me, please

A Meeting With My Mind

CHOCOLATE CITY

Let's get down to business

I mean, let's get down to the nitty-gritty

Lay back, relax, kick off your shoes

Let's take a ride thru Chocolate City

When you tune into Chocolate City

Leave all your worries behind

Because when you cruise thru Chocolate City

It's guaranteed to blow your mind

Let the music make your body move

Let the sound take you to new heights

People tune in from miles away

To get a dose of Chocolate City every day and night

From midnight to midnight, believe me, it's the thing to do

A dose of Chocolate City is what I recommend to all of you

The sounds you hear will definitely set your mind free

89.9 on your radio dial is where you want to be

Jazz, blues, poetry, and a little bit of news

Information on all the artists, tell me how can you lose?

Believe me, Chocolate City is sweet music to your ears

No rap or heavy metal in Chocolate City, no music to fear

Meet the mayor of Chocolate City, a brotha that's smooth as ice

Keeping the music flowing and never playing the same song twice

Chocolate City can only be found on your FM dial

The show with jazz, pizzazz, phat, and all that, with a one-of-a-kind style

CHAPTER SEVEN
LOVE

TEARS OF A BROKEN HEART

Why Is it so hard to understand?

Can anybody explain why?

How do you control your emotions,

Once a broken heart begins to cry?

Can you consider yourself human,

If you don't show sorrow and pain?

Once a broken heart begins to cry

The feeling can drive you insane

I hope you don't have to experience it

Or should I say it's something you should fear?

Once a broken heart begins to cry

You can't control your tears

I can try to describe the feeling to you

I'm sure it will take me all-day

Once a broken heart begins to cry

There's really not much you can say

I'll tell you from experience

Your eyes won't stay very dry

Once a broken heart begins to cry

A Meeting With My Mind

BOX FULL OF LOVE

Dear God, above, I have a few things to say

Hopefully, you can hear me as I kneel down and pray

Send down some blessings, high from above

And on the package, label it, "A box full of love."

Please bless our leaders throughout the entire world

Bless all your creation, bless man, woman, boy, and girl

We're lacking lots of love down here; society is really mean

The National Anthem should have been Dr. King's speech, "I Have a Dream."

I, too, have a dream that one day, I just don't know when

This world will be full of love, and there'll be no such thing as sin

Everyone will come together, joining hand in hand

I know God can make it happen because I heard you're the man

I know that's asking a lot; perhaps that's a great big task

We all know you can do it, then it's up to us to make it last

Some call you a leader; to me, you're the leader of the pack

I hope I'm one of the blessed ones because I heard you're coming back

I know I'm one in a million asking for the same thing

God, you know why we ask? Because of the happiness, you bring

You're the greatest role model in the world; many lives you've inspired

I know you're blessing us 24-7, but please, God, don't get tired

I'm asking for these blessings, God; I heard you're always around

I don't have everything I've asked for still; you've never let me down

Send the blessings by train, plane, or on the wings of a snow-white dove

Send them by Federal Express or UPS, God, we really need that

Box full of love

BOYFRIENDS

Boyfriends will come, boyfriends will go

Some relationships will die out, some will grow

Some will be there to help you get through your greatest fears

Some will be a contributing factor when you release your tears

Some will offer support or, should I say, lend a helping hand

Some you will be able to relate to, some you will never understand

Some will leave you hanging, some will never be there for you

Some will be so unfair; some will even be true

Some will buy you nothing, some will buy you fancy clothes

Some will caress your entire body, some will even lick your toes

Some will offer solutions to solving your heartbreaks

Some will be the aspirin to cure all your headaches

BURN BABY BURN

I want to write a poem about "love."
Unfortunately, I don't know where to start
You see, I've been in love so many times before
So many times, I end up with a broken heart
I mean, I put my all in all into it
Only to be let down in return
If I could bag up all the heartaches I've had
I'd set it on fire and let it burn, baby burn

BUSTED AND DISGUSTED

As she sat outside honking and honking her horn

The signal for me to come on out, it's time to go,

"Go"

Oh yeah, it's nine o'clock; less than an hour ago, I told her I loved her

But, within that hour, another young lady came over unexpected

Earlier in the day, I told her I loved her too

I guess it's raining too hard outside for her to get out of the car

Thank God for the rain

As she drives off, I'm already thinking of an excuse to tell her

But this other young lady is distracting my thoughts or my lies

Now the phone starts to ring off the hook

Damn, I thought I turned the ringer off

Who the fuck could that be?

I don't remember telling anyone else I love them today

Please, baby, come back, bitch, please go home, please caller, get off my line

CLAUDIA

C is for "Caring"

Something I always do

L is for "Love"

My "love "is very true.

A is for "Always"
"Always" being there.

U is for "Understanding"
And showing how much, I care.

D is for "Destiny"
Not knowing how far

I is for "Individual."
For I am a shining star

A is for "Awesome"
That I tend to be
These are the meanings of my name
And there's no other way to describe "me."

DADDY'S LITTLE GIRL

Here I sit all alone

Been like this since my daddy been gone

I forgive my daddy for what he did

The judge and jury gave my daddy a lifetime bid

I'll never get to ask my daddy for money

He's been sentenced to life, so nothing to me is funny

He'll never get to see me ride my bike

I'm writing him letters, but in jail, they're called kites

Daddy, I'm the captain of the city drill team

Why did the judicial system have to be so mean?

Daddy, I wish you were here to see me play softball

Instead of being locked inside those concrete walls

I wish you were here to teach me how to drive

Even though you're locked up, I'm glad you're still alive

Daddy, I read and respond to all your letters

I know if you were here, things would be a lot better

Daddy, I want you to know I'm in church every Sunday

I'm also the first one up for school every Monday

Even though you'll never get to drop me off at school

I'm going to do as you said and live by the "Golden Rule."

"Do unto others as you would have others do unto you."

You told me to love everybody and love myself too.

A Meeting With My Mind

You told me to always do my best and say no to drugs

As I sit here crying, Daddy, I wish you were here to give me a hug

I'm going to do my best, Daddy, in school and strive for all "A's."

And as I get older, I'm going to change all my negative ways

Daddy, one day I'm going to graduate and go straight to college

And as always, you told me to consume all the knowledge

I'll never look at myself as being a minority

Instead, to be a strong Black woman will be my priority

The judge and jury don't know what it's like being left alone

If they gave you another chance, I'd make sure you'd stay home

I'd scream and holler every time you touched the door

Daddy to keep you home, I would fall out on the floor

Daddy, I want you to know every night, I kneel and pray

That God will protect you in there to be with me another day

You have three strikes; they gave you life; what more can they really do?

You're my daddy always and forever, and I'll never turn my back on you

I'll remember Daddy, knowledge is the key in this cruel, cruel world

Even though you're not here with me, Daddy, I'll always be Daddy's little girl

DON'T MESS WITH MINE

Would I be less of a man if I didn't help this man up, who has fallen down?

Even if I was the cause of this man being on the ground

Should I tell this man I'm sorry, even though it was no mistake?

Should I really care about his pains or even his headaches?

Do you think I should care if, for some reason, his bones I had to break?

Did he not know my courage was tested; my manhood was at stake?

Should I shake his hand, or would I be wrong to tip my hat

Should I let someone tell him I'm not going out like that?

If put in that same situation again, I'd do the same thing next time

Mess with any other lady in the world, but please don't mess with mine

JUST FOR YOU VICKY

This poem is for a special lady named Vicky
Who just happens to be my wife
Hopefully, I pray each and every day
That with her I'll spend the rest of my life
Over the years, I've written poems for friends
I've written poems for family members too
Now, after a thousand poems or so
Vicky, I'm writing this one just for you
Vicky, you mean the world to me
Like the song says, "you're one in a million."
If I had to place a dollar value on you, dear,
Let's see, it would be somewhere in the billions
We've shared so many good times together
We've stood by each other through thick and thin
I mean, even during the bad times, we stuck it out
Damn, Baby, you're like my very best friend
We've both made our mistakes in life
But somehow, we stuck together to work them out
Still, through it all, there we stand hand in hand
I guess that's what "love" is all about
Not only have you been a beautiful wife to me
You've been a wonderful mother to all our kids

A Meeting With My Mind

Somehow in that big, beautiful heart of yours

You've forgiven me for some of the wrong I did

If I searched this world from sea to sea

I'm sure there would be no other

Who could show and give me the love you have

Vicky, I place your love up there with God and my mother

Vicky, you've been my backbone, my guiding light

When some of my so-called friends went astray

And in my heart, don't let anyone tell you different

Is where you will always and forever stay

So, as I bring this poem to an end

I pray that we will always be together

Vicky, "I love you" more than words can say

And I'm going to keep on loving you forever and ever.

A Meeting With My Mind

FEMALE JIVE TALK

I watched him through the window as he stepped out of his car

Wondering will I get a chance to be his lucky star

I'm sitting at the bar chilling as he strolled through the door

My eyes on him like a radar as he hit the dance floor

He's fine as wine, suave should I say, like a trophy on a shelf

I can't believe a man so fine is at the nightclub by himself

Smooth face, sideburns trimmed, girl, he was so fine

Bartender, send that man another drink on me, the most expensive glass of wine

His suit was made of silk, matching shoes, with long curly hair

Call me a stalker, but girl, I can't help but stare

Girl, let me tell you, if he were mine, I'd buy him anything

He was all that. Ladies, please step back; I'd even buy the wedding rings

Bobbing my head to the sounds of this funky jazz band

Girl, wouldn't it be nice if I could walk over and grab his hand

If this were a beauty pageant, he'd walk away with the grand prize

With that hard rock sexy body and those sparkles in his eyes

Excuse me, waiter, check this out. Send that man another drink

I can't let him out of my sight, girl; I'm scared to even blink

Girl, I better step to him while I still have a chance

I want to ask him, is there any way possible, I can have the next dance?

Lights dimmed, music was just right; yeah, it's time to groove

I couldn't have picked a better time or place; it's time to make my move

I leaned over and whispered to him, "what does a lady like me have to do

To get your number, a dinner date, or just spend a little time with you?"

He said, "just be real, be yourself, and everything will be alright."

He said, "thanks for the dance and the drinks; let's hook up tomorrow night."

I said, "you got a date" girl, I couldn't wait to see this man again

He gave me his number, address too, said he'd pick me up at ten

He walked me to my car, gave me a big kiss, and told me he had a nice time

Girl, now I got to do everything I can to make this man all mine.

FRIENDS

Friends are hard to find these days; you can answer that yourself

"True friends" should be cherished like trophies on a shelf

Friends don't come easy; just take a look around

"True friends" are measured by the ounces, never by the pound

Friends will be there for you when the going gets too tough

"True friends" will ride out the storm with you when the water seems so rough

Friends will never forsake you; now, that's what I call loyalty

"True Friends" deserve to be treated like royalty

Friends will pick you up when they see you have fallen down

"True friends" will try to catch you before you hit the ground

Friends will be there for you in your time of need

"True friends" will look for nothing in return if they assist you in a good deed

Friends will lead the way if, for some reason, you should get lost

"True friends" can't be bought whatever may be the cost

Friends will clear a path for you when obstacles get in your way

"True friends" will be there to hold and comfort you on your darkest day

Friends will sit and talk with you when you're feeling down and out

"True friends" will refer you to Jesus; his advice you cannot doubt

Friends will take a joint effort approach that includes you and me

"True friends" will make a "friendship" last through love, peace, and harmony

A Meeting With My Mind

HAPPY BIRTHDAY MOTHER

Well, well, well, this one's especially for you, my dear mother

You're the sweetest mother in the world. Believe me, there is no other

If I searched this world from coast to coast, from sea to shining sea

There's not another mother on this planet; Mama, you are the one for me

I've searched the whole United States; I even took a ride up to space

I still wasn't able to find someone, anyone, mother to take your place

I left space, went to China, then went over to Japan

Then, I went over to Africa. I even shook Winnie Mandela's hand

From Africa, I went to England to spend some time with the Queen

I told her all about you, Mama, she said she knows exactly what I mean

She said she heard all about you, Mama; I told her you're worth more than a bag of pearls

I said Queen, you're "Goddamn right" I wouldn't trade her for nothing in the world

I left England and went to Spain. They sent me over to Rome

They told me no one compares to your mother. She can even sit on the King's throne

They asked me if I had been to Canada, and I told them, "No, not yet."

I'm sure if they ever met my mother, they'd give her the utmost respect

She's one in a million; believe me, she's worth her weight in gold

1000 pounds of silver couldn't replace her; please let the story be told

So let me get back to the United States because I'm just tired of looking

I've eaten at the finest restaurants worldwide, none compare to mom's home-style cooking

Mother, if it wasn't for your guidance, I'm more than sure I'd be lost

You've shared so much good advice; that's why you're my boss

So Mother, as I bring this journey to an end, please just let me say

I love you with all my heart, and Mother, have a beautiful birthday

I APOLOGIZE

You stayed out all night. You didn't even call.

I stayed up all night staring at your picture on the wall

I waited by the phone all night, but still no ring

Still, I lay and wait for you despite all the tears you bring

I can't understand you, baby; why are you treating me so bad

I remember the day you told me I was the best thing you ever had

My friends say you're playing me, and that may be so true

I feel you're doing me wrong, but I'm still waiting for you

Baby, I'm getting tired. I can't take these silly games

A lady called here this morning and asked for you by name

Still, I keep my fingers crossed, praying to the heavens above

Hoping that you come back to me because it's you that I really love

IF YOU LET ME

If you let me, I'll insert a seed inside your heart and raise it with care

If you let me, I'll nurture the seed with all my heart and promise to be fair

If you let me, I'll cultivate the seed; I swear I'll make the seed grow

If you let me, I'll separate you in the "Garden of Love," I'd give you your own row

If you let me, I'll fertilize the seed with more love if you keep that to yourself

If you let me, I'll give you plenty of sunshine, but you can't tell anyone else

If you let me, I'll landscape the seed every day; you'd stand out from all the rest

If you let me, I'll water you morning, noon, and night to show you are the best

If you let me, I'll sing to you under the moon, but please excuse my voice

If you let me, I'll put you in a flowerpot because you're my #1 choice

If you let me, I'll caress the seed to the highest heights of ecstasy

If you let me, I'll tattoo the seed on my chest; you really mean that much to me

I'LL GET THERE

I'll get there by plane, train, or automobile

Darling, for you, I'll sail the rough tides of the sea

I'll do whatever it takes to get me there

With you is truly where I want to be

I need you by my side at night

I need to see your beautiful face when I wake

Darling, I'll get there by plane, train, or automobile

For you, I'll swim the ocean waters if that's what it takes

I need to be there to hold your hand

As we stroll together on the wet sands of the beach

Even though we're thousands of miles apart

Darling, you're still within my reach

I'll get there through rain, shine, sleet, or snow

I'll get there regardless of the weather

There will be no reason in this whole wide world

That will keep the two of us from being together

I'll get there by plane, train, or automobile

For you, Darling, I'll part the red sea

I'll do all these things because I love you, Darling

You really mean that much to me

I'M SORRY, BABY

Since you left, baby

My life has not been the same

I guess this is how it feels

When you're going insane

I can't sleep at night

Tossing and turning in my bed

I miss you so much, baby

I just can't get you out of my head

I've been so lonely, baby

Now that you're finally gone

It's such a hurting feeling

Now that I'm all alone

If you come back to me, baby

I swear no more fussing or fights

Baby, I miss you most

When day turns into night

I miss your beautiful smile

I miss your beautiful face

No one in this entire world

Could ever take your place

The lovely walks on the beach

You and I, hand in hand

A Meeting With My Mind

Me calling you my lady

And you calling me your man

I'm sorry, baby

IN THE EYES OF THE BEHOLDER

It's been said beauty is in the eyes of the beholder

This quote is so very true

You see, my heart skipped a beat

The minute I laid eyes on you

I heard so much about your beauty

I just had to see for myself

And yes, I must admit

Your beauty is like a trophy on a shelf

When you smile, it's like the sunshine

A gleam so very bright

The beauty you possess, dear

Can turn darkness into light

Your beautiful long black hair

Oh, how I long to run my fingers through it

I mean, your beauty knocks me off my feet

Ask of me anything dear, and I'll do it

You see, it's said beauty is in the eyes of the beholder

I can truly say your beauty is ocean deep

Therefore, I'd climb the highest mountain

It's because of your beauty I'd take this leap

MISSING YOU MARIO PLASCENCIA

December 18th, I'll never forget
What a day to remember in my life
We stood hand in hand; you became my husband
I became your beautiful wife

I'll never forget the day I first saw you
It was "love at first sight."
And now, thinking back on that day
The feeling was so, so very right

At the bus station, I sat watching you
Never thinking we would become "one."
I thank you for leaving me with God's greatest creation
David and Mario, our two handsome sons

I remember you used to call them your babies
They are still my babies, that they are
And through them, I see you, Mario
For you are still my shining star

A Meeting With My Mind

But now, Mario, I find myself feeling down

All alone and so broken-hearted

Mario, I must confess my life just has not been the same

Since you dearly departed

My heart cries for you daily, Mario

And without you, there's such an empty space

Mario, if I lived another 1000 years

No other man will ever take your place

I'm always thinking about the good times we shared, Mario

I think about the bad times too

God knows I would do anything in this world, Mario

To share them again with you

I remember all the joy and happiness we shared, Mario

But without you, joy and happiness is hard to find

Even though you are not here with me, baby

Mario, every day of the year, you're on my mind

I think about all the fun we had together as a family, Mario

All the good times we spent together

That's something I can hold on 'til my dying day, Mario

Because memories last forever

A Meeting With My Mind

The kids and I miss you so very much, Mario

We would do anything to have you near

Yet, I try to be strong for David and Mario

Both you and I would not want them to fear

I will always put forth the effort to remain strong

For, I know that's what you would want me to do

When I'm feeling down, Mario, just the thought of you

Makes me feel brand new

I still love you unconditionally, Mario

And I would not have it any other way.

I'm speaking to you, Mario, as if you were right here

So, baby, believe every word I say

When times get hard, Mario, I look up to the heavens

For you to help me make it through the day

Hoping and praying you are watching over us

And wondering, if you were here, what would you say

Would you be saying I'm doing a great job?

Being a mother to our kids

Would you still love, honor, and respect me, Mario?
The same way you always did?

You see, Mario, God called you home for a reason
And that was his call to make
Maybe he needed a big strong angel up in heaven
So, it was you, Mario, he decided to take

Sometimes it seems like the world is on my back
And the weight I can no longer bare
But I keep pushing Mario because I feel your presence
This lets me know you're always there

In my heart, you'll stay forever, Mario
Forever in my heart, you'll always be
In my heart, there'll never be another Mario
It will always and forever be you and me

The last time we saw each other at the airport
I was so sad when we hugged and you said goodbye
I asked you, please don't say goodbye to me that way
That word alone just made me cry

Not only were you my husband, Mario

You were a father and also my best friend

If I could live my life all over

I would do anything to share it with you again

As I end, I pray that you keep watching over me and the kids, Mario

High from the heavens above

And I'll always remember your last words to me

When you said, "see you soon, my love."

Love you, Mario, always and forever,

Myra

MASTER PLAN

Sitting at home all by myself

Staring at your pictures on the bedroom shelf

You've been gone now for a couple of years

Still, I fight to hold back the tears

I continue to tell myself enough is enough

I didn't know, Pops, life was going to be so rough

When you were living, I knew everything would be alright

You taught me how to overcome fear and fight

Man Pops, I just miss you being around

You taught me how to get back up in life whenever I fell down

Having you as a Pops was such a thrill

And from you, Pops, I learned how to pay my bills

It was you who taught me about the "facts of life."

How to raise my children and respect my wife

You taught me things I did not know

Simple things like when to say yes and when to say no

You made me the person I am today, and that's no doubt

Thank you, Pops, for showing me what life was all about

You showed me the right way how to be a real man

Thanks, Pops, for leaving me with a "master plan."

See you when I get there.

MY FIRST KISS

I remember when I was a little boy

I closed my eyes and made a wish

I wished that one day, someway, somehow

My playground sweetheart would give me a big kiss

You see, I heard about this kiss thing before

I even saw it done on tv.

I wondered how I could get my playground sweetheart

To accept a kiss from me

See, we played on the merry-go-round together

We even pushed each other on the swings

Sometimes, I would make her laugh so hard

When I tried too hard to sing

We played hopscotch, jump rope, and ate mud cakes together

My playground sweetheart was the joy of my little life

And when it rained, we stayed in and played house

I was the husband, and of course, she was my wife

I knew we could never be married right now

Besides, we were both ways too young

But there was nothing wrong with pretending

Besides, we both were having so much fun

I protected her on the playground with all my heart

You see, to me, she was my playground queen

A Meeting With My Mind

And I bought her the biggest fake gold diamond ring

To ever come out of a 25-cent bubble gum machine

Then one day, we met on the playground again

Alone, just the two of us underneath the monkey bars

She gently grabbed my little hands, and I fainted

Inside, my head was full of stars

My heart was beating 100 miles per hour

A baby heart attack was well within reach

You could tell I was very nervous

It was obvious in my speech

I gave her a rose I hid behind my back

She told me to close my eyes and make a wish

She looked both ways and puckered up

And upon my cheek gave me my first big kiss

MY MOTHER TOLD ME

God, times are really hard down here

It seems there is no one I can turn to

My mother has always told me

In times like these, I can always turn to you

I find that statement to be so real

That's why I turn to you time and time again

A Meeting With My Mind

And you will forgive me for all my sins

She told me always put God first in my life

Leave all my worries behind

My mother told me to talk to you when times get rough

She promised me, in you, I'd find peace of mind

She said when it seems like I can't take any more

Mother told me to take all my worries to the altar and leave them there

She told me, God, you are a great God

For you would never leave me in despair

My mother told me if God can't fix it, son, it couldn't be fixed

All power are in your hands

Throughout my life, my mother has never steered me wrong

I can only say God, she was right; you are truly "the Man."

NO OTHER WAY

Heavenly Father, I come to you today

For you are the king of my life

Not only have you walked hand in hand with me

You've been there through all my stress and strife

I'll never place a man above you, Father

No man on earth has ever done what you have done

You gave your life so we may have life

You even gave us your only begotten son

Father, you've shared all my trials and tribulations

As a man, I can ask for no more

For I walk by faith, not by sight

Never knowing what the next day has in store

Father, you've never placed too many burdens on me

Should I say no more than my body could bear?

And when my ways seemed weary.

You stepped in to show me you cared

There are still those who don't believe in you

To each, his own is all I can say

You are everything in this world to me, dear Father

Father, I would not have it any other way

SEA DREAMS

As I sit at the dock of the bay, my mind begins to dream

The weather begins to change, and the seagulls begin to scream

The sun begins to set as the day turns to night

The ocean breeze blows out the candles then comes the moonlight

All that's missing is you, dear as a tear falls from my eye

Baby, you light up my heart like the stars light up the night sky

Can you please forgive me, baby? Please give me one more chance

Let me hold and squeeze you one more time, just one last slow dance

I'm so lost without you, for you mean so much to me

I'll be waiting for your ship to come in as I sit and dream of you by the sea

SEXCAPADE

When I'm all alone and all by myself

I think about you and nothing else

I think about what could have been

And wonder will it ever happen again

I remember that night all too good

Baby, I wouldn't trade that feeling if I could

Could another man ever make me feel that way?

Ladies, that kind of loving, would make any woman pay

I remember the exact minute it all began

A Meeting With My Mind

It was a Tuesday night, approximately five minutes to ten

We talked, had wine, and then came the first kiss

Girlfriend, I closed my eyes and made a wish

He stroked his fingers through my hair

Unstrapped my bra, and off came my underwear

"Yes, you can, baby" was the last words I said

My dress fell to the floor as we climbed in bed

He started off by gently rubbing my back

He told me not to worry, just lay back and relax

He rubbed me down with lotion, his body I began to caress

Suddenly, his luscious lips landed upon my breast

I began to weaken, then all of a sudden

I felt his tongue circling my belly button

I reached up to wipe the sweat from my nose

He raised my legs, kissed my feet, and began to suck my toes

Then he placed his hips between my thighs

Girl, it felt so good it made me cry

As he moved his body up and down

"Oooohhh baby" was my only sound

He rolled over and positioned me on top

It's 1:30 am, and now I'm begging him to stop

And when that time finally came

He covered my mouth as I exhaled and screamed out his name

For the rest of my life, that's one night I'll always treasure

He apologized for all the pain, but I thanked him for all the pleasure

TRUE LOVE

Can you tell me you really love me?

If you look into my eyes

Together can we seek the brightest star

That awaits us in the sky

Tell me this is true love

As I fight to hold back the tears

Will you be the one for me now?

And or the next 100 years

Will we love, honor, and respect one another?

For the rest of our life

Can we truly abide by the wedding vows?

Should we become husband and wife?

I know you are the only one for me

Because you are always in my dreams

I hope that doesn't sound too realistic

Me and you becoming a team

We'll sail the 7 seas together, baby

Just you and me

Together, forever me and you as one

Is how it will always and forever be?

UNITY

Love is beautiful when it comes from within

Unity is greater because that's where it all begins

Join together, make one, become one means unite

Unity means oneness no matter if you're black or white

It has a significant meaning that applies to all races

Unity can bring smiles to all frowning faces

You can start unity in the home, on the job, or in the school

Unity should have been part of man's golden rule

Unity is not confined to one area unity can roam from place to place

Unity brought two countries together even though they met in space

How does it feel to be mistreated because of the color of your skin?

Unity can conquer that problem that way, we all win

One for all and all for one

Unity brings happiness, and happiness turns into fun

Together we stand, divided we fall

Unity brings us together, together means all

I WANT TO BE

This year I'll be another year older. I was really looking forward to it until I ran into you. We laughed and chatted, but before we said our goodbyes, you asked, "What do you want to be?" I said to be the girl who knows she's worth it. I want to be the girl who knows her worth, the arguments, the yelling, and the screaming. I wanna be worth the tears and the sadness, the laughter, and the happiness. I want to be the girl who gets asked, "how was your day?" Not because you know if I don't have a good day, then you won't have a good day either. I want to be the girl who's loved, not the way you love your mother or your daughter or even your sister. I want the kind of love that is special, that no one else can have. It's endless. I want to be all that and more; I want to be worth all that and more. So, next time you see me, you won't have to ask what I want to be. You will know, you will feel, you will understand. I won't have to tell you twice because I will be that girl who knows I'm more than worth it.

WHY DID YOU LIE?

Why did you lie to me at the chapel when you said you love me?

Why did you lie when you said you would place no one above me?

Why did you lie about our future? Was it the right thing to do?

Why did you lie to me when you said you would forever be true?

Why did you lie? I mean, do you really think that was right?

Why did you lie to me, saying it felt so good the other night?

Why did you lie when you told me you would always be part of my tomorrow?

Why did you lie to me when you said until death you would never cause sorrow?

Why did you lie when you said no other man would ever take my place?

Why did you lie when you said you would never bring tears to my face?

Why did you lie to me when you swore, we would never be a part?

Why did you lie to me when you said you would never break my heart?

CHAPTER 8
MELODIES OF LIFE AND LOVE

A Meeting With My Mind

NEVER GONNA STOP

You stayed out all night

You didn't even call

I stayed up all night

Staring at your picture on the wall

I waited by the phone

But there was no ring

Still, I laid and waited for you

Despite all the tears you bring

Hook:

I'm never gonna stop, never gonna stop, never gonna stop loving you

I'm never gonna stop, never gonna stop, never gonna stop loving you

I can't understand, baby.

Why you treat me so bad

I remember you told me

I was the sweetest lady you ever had

My friends say you're playing me

And that may be true

You're doing me wrong

But I'm still waiting for you

Hook:

I'm never gonna stop, never gonna stop, never gonna stop loving you

I'm never gonna stop, never gonna stop, never gonna stop loving you

Baby, I'm getting tired.

Tired of all your silly games

A lady called here this morning

She asked for you by name

She told me you were her man

And it's driving me insane

But I guess with all the love

There has to be some pain

Hook:

I'm never gonna stop, never gonna stop, never gonna stop loving you

I'm never gonna stop, never gonna stop, never gonna stop loving you

A Meeting With My Mind

NEVER LET YOU GO

Baby, when I think of you, I get chills up and down my spine
The thought of having someone that's so, so very fine
I find myself thinking about you, morning, noon, and night
And when we're making love, I squeeze your body so very tight
So, listen, baby, there's something I want you to know
That I don't never, ever, never want to let you go

Never, ever, never let you go.
Never, ever, never let you go.
Never, ever, never let you go.

These feelings I have for you get stronger every day
And if I had 10 wishes, I wouldn't want it any other way
The way you make love to me is like a roller coaster ride
Up and down, round and round, and I'm still right by your side
Like two love birds, you and I go hand and hand
And I'm committed to being your one and only man

Never, ever, never let you go.
Never, ever, never let you go.
Never, ever, never let you go.

So, baby, this song is for you and only you. Without you in my life, tell me what I would do?

It's a serious situation, but I can play this game

And in between the sheets, you make me scream out your name

I wouldn't trade you in, baby, if I could

You hold me right, squeeze me tight, and make me feel so good.

Never, ever, never let you go.

Never, ever, never let you go.

Never, ever, never let you go.

MISSING YOU

Hook:

Missing you, yes, I'm missing you

Missing you, missing you

Missing you, yes, I'm missing you

Missing you, missing you

Since you left me

My life hasn't been the same

I guess this is how it feels

When you're going insane

I can't sleep at night

A Meeting With My Mind

Tossing and turning in my bed
I miss you so much, baby
I just can't get you out of my head

Hook:
Missing you, yes, I'm missing you
Missing you, missing you
Missing you, yes, I'm missing you
Missing you, missing you

I've been so lonely
Now that you're gone
It's such a hurting feeling
Now that I'm alone
If you come back to me
No more fussing or fights
Baby, I miss you most
When day turns into night
Hook:
Missing you, yes, I'm missing you
Missing you, missing you
Missing you, yes, I'm missing you
Missing you, missing you

I miss those smile

You put on my face

No one in this world

Could ever take your place

The walks on the beach

You and I, hand in hand

You calling me your lady

And me calling you my man

Hook:
Missing you, yes, I'm missing you

Missing you, missing you

Missing you, yes, I'm missing you

Missing you, missing you

MY MAN

I remember the first day

When you came and sat next to

I thought to myself

How lucky can a young lady be?

All alone, all by yourself

Just me and you

Baby, was this a dream

Or a fairytale come true

How could I be so, so lucky

I just don't understand

I want to be your lady; please be my man

I want to be your lady, and will you please be my man?

I want to be your lady, and will you please be my man?

I want to be your lady, and will you please be my man?

(Rap)

Girls, I wish you knew him. I love to do him

No, I am not feeling any shame

And if you had a man that could love you this way

I'm sure you would say the same

You asked me out on a date

Now, how could I ever say no?

Baby, I'm yours and all yours

Take me wherever you want me to go

You got me under a love spell

Your wish is my command

I get so weak at the knees

Every time you touch my hand

There's no way I would ever leave you

Even if I could

Because the love we make every night

Is just so, so good

I want to be your lady, and will you please be my man?

I want to be your lady, and will you please be my man?

I want to be your lady, and will you please be my man?

A Meeting With My Mind

KNOCK KNOCK

Knock, knock, who's there? It's me. Can you just let me in?

Knock, knock, who's there? It's me. Can you just let me in?

The sun rose this morning. Now it's going down.

I'd just like to say thank you, God, for keeping me around

I've heard great things about you, even though you've never been seen

I heard living is great up there; down here, society is really mean

I don't know exactly where you are, I have a feeling you're always near

I wear a crucifix around my neck to lessen my fear

Knock, knock, who's there? It's me. Can you just let me in?

Knock, knock, who's there? It's me. Can you just let me in?

They tell me the streets up there are paved with gold, a place where everyone cares.

I don't have a lot to offer down here, but what I do have, I'm willing to share

I heard you've been answering prayers up there since the beginning of time

I pray that you protect me down here from being a victim of a violent crime

I wish I was up there; I heard it's beautiful, and there isn't any air pollution

A Meeting With My Mind

With millions of people down here, we still haven't found that right solution

Knock, knock, who's there? It's me. Can you just let me in?
Knock, knock, who's there? It's me. Can you just let me in?

I read about the angels flying around and all the beautiful white doves
I know what the world is lacking down here. It's simple, "love."
I know the burden is heavy, God because everyone depends on you
I don't know anyone else to turn to, so what am I to do
I look for you daily as I stare into the bright blue sky
I thank you for blessing me to see another day, but still, I ask, "why?"

Knock, knock, who's there? It's me. Can you just let me in?
Knock, knock, who's there? It's me. Can you just let me in?

I haven't lived a perfect life; I admit I've committed sin
If somehow, I make it up there and knock on the door, please just let me in.

RAINDROP TEARS

Raindrops are falling
Down my window pain
Since we broke up
Nothing seems the same
I can't sleep at night
So, what am I to do?
I squeeze my pillow so tight at night
Thinking that it's you

Hook:
Like the rain outside
My tears keep falling
And in the middle of the night
It's your name I'm calling

I made some big mistakes.
I know I can never erase
Now within my heart
There's such an empty space
I haven't felt this way
Since you walked out my life
You promised me that one day

We would be husband and wife

Hook:
Like the rain outside
My tears keep falling
And in the middle of the night
It's your name I'm calling

Please can we make it work??
Can we get back together?
I want out in my life.
Forever and ever
My friends talk behind my back
But baby, I don't care
My family tried to tell me
That it's just not fair

Hook:
Like the rain outside
My tears keep falling
And in the middle of the night
It's your name I'm calling

I should leave you alone.

And just walk away

But without you by my side at night

I can't live another day

I think I'm going crazy; they say I'm going insane

Baby, I miss the way

You mix the pleasure with the pain

Hook:

Like the rain outside

My tears keep falling

And in the middle of the night

It's your name I'm calling

A Meeting With My Mind

UPTIGHT LOVE AFFAIR

Lately, I've been feeling so uptight

Your body's calling me in the middle of the night

Sexual fantasies running through my head

I got a special place reserved for you in my bed

Let me sex you up. I'll make you feel fine

2, 3, 4, 5, 69 times

Hook

It's you that I need; it's you that I'm missing

I keep my fingers crossed and keep wishing

That you quit playing games and be for real

I'm giving it my all; now it's your call; tell me, what's the deal?

Like Keith Sweat said, "something, something, something just ain't right."

I used to go to your house any time of the night.

Hook

Now you're telling me to call before I come

I may be stupid for your love, but I'm not dumb

I'm phoning for your love because I know you got it going on

I left 10 messages on your machine saying, please call me when you get home

You're a freak by nature; that's what I've been told

I'm checking my 2-way every minute looking for your code

Hook

Sent a dozen roses to your job, and they sent them back

I'm going door to door looking for you, baby. Where you at?

Baby, where you at? I need you in my life.

I want you to be my girl forever; I want you to be my wife

I'm going crazy without you, baby. I need to see your face

No other girl in this whole wide world could take your place

Hook

CHAPTER NINE
PAIN

A Meeting With My Mind

PLEASE MR. DOPEMAN

I remember when Moms used to give me hugs

Now, she's asking me for drugs

She's staying up all day and night

Crack cocaine is taking away her life

I wonder what Moms will do next

For a small piece of crack cocaine, she'll give you sex

Neighborhood Rat is her new name

Dope man got my Moms turning tricks, and he's feeling no shame

My Moms is stuck in your crack house for three long days

It's sad no one in my family can change her ways

Dope man, you've taken my Moms down the wrong path

It's been almost a week, and Moms hasn't taken a bath

I heard she asked the neighbor did she have a comb to spare

Now that Moms is on crack, she won't even comb her hair

Moms is running around the neighborhood with no shoes on her feet

Moms has lost a lot of weight because she has no time to eat

She don't care about lunch, dinner, or breakfast

Dope man is wearing my Moms gold necklace

I remember all the joy Moms used to bring

Word around the hood is she smoked off her wedding ring

Moms once had dreams of becoming a movie star

Now that she's on crack, she'll turn a trick in the back seat of a car

A Meeting With My Mind

I remember Moms told me, "Son, don't be a drug abuser."

Now around the hood, she's known as an "any drug" user

Moms used to be highly respected; that's no doubt

Before the Dope Man and his crack turned her out

I remember Moms used to wear a beautiful bright smile on her face

My sisters are embarrassed of her; my brothers say Moms is a disgrace

I wish I could tell her Moms at home is where you really need to be

The Dope Man has even got our floor model tv.

They tell me Moms is real sick and she's got a real bad cough

I can't call for help because our phone is turned off

Believe it or not, Moms used to be a high school teacher

"Please, will you pray for my Moms?" is what I ask the preacher

Dope Man, Dope Man, please hear my call; I don't want you to see me cry

Dope Man, I want to talk to you when these tears stop falling from my eyes

Then, I know God will pick up the slack

Please, I'm begging you, Mr. Dope Man, can I please have my Moms back?

SEX SEX SEX

Is that all you can talk about is SEX SEX SEX
Who's the lucky victim? I mean, who will be next
Can't even concentrate; SEX is the only thing on your mind
You say when it comes to SEX SEX SEX, you're color blind
You say when it comes to SEX SEX SEX, you aim to please
You don't even think twice about catching a venereal disease
You say SEX SEX SEX is in with the "X" generation
To top it off, you're having SEX SEX SEX unprotected
You always got a SEX SEX SEX story to sell or tell
Bragging about how much money you spent on the motel
Twelve years in school and is that all you learned in class.
SEX SEX SEX, sorry, no thank you, I think I'll pass

TIRED TIMES

I'm tired of living life like this

Sometimes, I want to give up

They say it runneth over

But there's nothing in my cup

Life just seems so unfair

And nobody gives a damn

I look in the mirror every day

And I still can't tell you who I am

I try to be a best friend to all my friends

That in itself is still not enough

The high tides of life seem so calm

But the fight for equal rights are so tough

I often wonder will times get better

Will times in this life ever change?

If I say thank you or you're welcome

Will society stop looking at me strangely?

One day this life will all be over

And "me" will be no more

I lived my whole life rich in spirit

But in reality, I'll leave here, poor

A Meeting With My Mind

WHO'S TO BLAME?

Who's to blame for this world's present situation? We may never know

Who's to blame when we're running out of patience and have nowhere to go?

Who's to blame for all the men and women that are in jail doing time?

Who's to blame for all the young juveniles that are now doing violent crimes?

Who's to blame for all the war vets that are sleeping on the streets?

Who's to blame for all the homeless people that have no food to eat?

Who's to blame for the failing health care systems while the elderly keep dying?

Who's to blame for the abused welfare system while hungry babies keep crying?

Who's to blame for the crooked police who protect the drug dealer's drugs?

Who's to blame for all the innocent people that are killed and being mugged?

Who's to blame for the economy that can't produce enough jobs?

Who's to blame for the young boy or girl who decides to go out and rob?

Who's to blame for poverty? We all know the rich people don't really care

Who's to blame for all the smog that is polluting the earth's air?

Who's to blame for all the deadly diseases present in the world today?

Who's to blame for all the missing children that have mysteriously gone astray?

A Meeting With My Mind

Who's to blame for all the broken-up homes, divorced husbands, and separated wives?

Who's to blame for all the wars that have taken so many lives

Who's to blame for all the Americans hooked on tobacco, alcohol, and cocaine?

Who's to blame when a person knowingly kills but, when caught, pleads insane?

Who's to blame for all the blue-collar crimes like tax evasion, fraud, and extortion

Who's to blame for the young girl with no family planning who chose to get an abortion?

Who's to blame for all the illegal dumping of all the sewage in the seven seas?

Who's to blame for all the lumberjacks that are cutting down nature's trees?

Who's to blame for all the damage that's being done to the world's ozone?

Who's to blame when the spaceship goes up, but then suddenly something goes wrong?

Who's to blame for all the budget cuts that are affecting our children's education?

Who's to blame for all the corruption that's going on in the police station?

Who's to blame for the aerospace departments that are having the big layoffs?

Who's to blame for all the judges that are taking the big payoffs?

Who's to blame for all the hard-working youngsters whose pay is minimum wage?

Who's to blame when some psychopath enters a store and goes into a shooting rage?

A Meeting With My Mind

Who's to blame for the lack of gun control that has homicide at an all-time high?

Who's to blame for the witnesses who go under oath and still lie?

Who's to blame for all the chemicals and pesticides that are secretly put in our foods?

Who's to blame when one minute you're happy, and the next minute you're in a bad mood?

So, can somebody please tell me who's to blame? Society should really be shamed.

Everybody's pointing the finger at one another, but nobody wants to take the blame.

A BUM RAP

I've been compared to many people in my life

Yesterday someone even called me a bum

That night I closed my eyes real tight

Trying to imagine what my life has become

I used to be highly respected in my city

People used to call me by my name

Now that I'm down and out on my luck

Even my own family tells me they're ashamed

Still, I walk with a smile on my face

What else can I really do?

Maybe I'll ask another bum under the bridge

Because I really don't have a clue

Have I really reached that point in my life?

Should I go out now and seek some aid?

Grab me a shopping basket and hustle some bottles and cans

Because I see that's how other bums get paid

Should I hold a sign and stand on the freeway exit

To see just who really cares?

Stop by if you'd like to lend a helping hand.

The way my life is going seems like I'll soon be there

But if I'm not there, I'm not far away

This I promise you

A Meeting With My Mind

I'll probably be hanging with the other bums

Because bums are humans too

KEEP HOPE ALIVE

A young boy approached me the other day

He said, "Excuse me, sir, do you have some spare change?"

I said, "Excuse me, son, do I know you?"

The young boy looked at me kind of strange.

The young boy said, "Sir, I'm down on my luck; all I need is a buck,

I would like to get something to eat."

The young boy did look like he was in desperate need

From his head down to his dirty feet

He said, "Sir, life isn't treating me fair right now,

I should have never run away from home."

The young boy said he comes from a large family

But on these mean streets, he's all alone

He said he's eating out of trash cans, sleeping in cars

Walking the streets all day and night

My only advice to this poor young boy

"Keep your head up. One day it's going to all be alright."

The young boy said, "Sir, if I would have obeyed my mother,

Listened to my father, who knows where I would be,

I remember one day I made my parents so mad,

A Meeting With My Mind

They said they wish they would have aborted me,

They said I'd probably grow up to be nothing

Which explains my present situation today

And from the looks of it, Sir, I hate to admit

Looks like these streets is where I'm going to stay."

THINKING TO MYSELF

Sometimes I sit back and think to myself

And suddenly, I begin to cry

I have these hidden pains deep inside

And honestly, I don't know why

I mean, I've had my share of ups and downs

Trials and tribulations are not hard to find

Sometimes I sit back and think hard

I truly think I be losing my mind

I haven't been all I could be, as they say

I haven't gotten the most out of my life

Although I've tried to be the best father to my kids

I haven't been the best husband to my wife

Sometimes I think, is this for real?

Or am I living in some fantasy land

Sometimes I sit back and think to myself

Is my wife seeing another man?

Could life really be this hard for me?

Even though I'm working hard every day

Could people really turn their backs on me?

Because I don't talk like them or walk a certain way

I'm constantly facing discrimination

Because my skin color is not the same

A Meeting With My Mind

Why is it that sometimes people talk behind my back?

And try to scandalize my name.

I do unto others as I would have others do unto me

They say that's the "Golden Rule."

Still, there are those that don't understand that

And try to play me for a fool

I do my part because I feel it's my duty

Besides, they say that's the "American Way."

Sometimes I sit back and think to myself

It's going to all be alright one day

CHAPTER TEN
POLITICALLY INCORRECT

AMERICA THE UGLY

America the beautiful; how false can that statement be?

It's said to be the home of the brave, but I don't know about land of the free.

Free to me means to soar like an eagle or fly like a hummingbird

Being Black in America, I'll never know the meaning of that word

They call me Black. My skin is brown, and so what am I to do

I can run, but I can't hide; when they say, "Uncle Sam wants you."

I was born this color, I'm going to die this color, and I can't change the color of my skin.

When I was young, I had no idea my skin would be a lifetime sin.

I've been treated badly all my life, but I still manage to carry on

Sometimes my life seems so hard I wish I was never born

I look back at my roots; my ancestors now rest in their graves

Take a few seconds and just try to imagine what it was really like being a slave

Picking cotton from sunrise to sunset, not even earning a dime

Hundreds of years later, some Americans now say that should have been a crime

You labeled me a felon, took away my rights, now I can't even vote

Years ago, Blacks had no rights but were still being hung by their throats

Whatever happened to equal rights? I guess that doesn't include me

If I had the same rights as whites, who knows where I would be

A Meeting With My Mind

A doctor, lawyer, congressman, or maybe a politician

Because I'm Black, the only thing it seems I can do is simply keep wishing

Wishing that America treats me right; just give me a fair chance

Besides thinking all Blacks are good for is to rap, singing, and dance

I've been called names like coon ass, jackass, or a no-good nigger

I've learned not to respond in violence; I simply let my pen be my trigger

I pull my pen and let the ink flow as I write down what's on my mind

When I was growing up, my mother always told me to always be kind

Kind and respectful to the opposite race, no matter what their color may be

I was also told to always be honest, and the truth shall set you free

The experiences I've had in my lifetime are one of a big fairytale

Being that my skin will always be black, America will always expect me to fail

I will not fail; I'm a strong Black man who refuses to give up or cry

Unfortunately, I'm going to stay this way today, tomorrow, and probably until the day I die

A Meeting With My Mind

TO WHOM IT MAY CONCERN

Dear political leaders, listen up.

I have a few things to say

I don't expect you to respond

Because you probably don't care anyway

I'm a young Black man who's had it rough

But still, I have a lot of patience

Can somebody please tell me?

How the world has gotten into such a terrible situation

Term after term, you'll make big promises

Saying what you plan to do

4 years later, it seems like nothing has changed

And now your term is through

You said if you're elected

You'll change that and give us this

3 years into your term

And you're still on top of your promise list

You promised if you were elected

You would fight to keep taxes down

Every year taxes keep rising

And you're nowhere around

Just elect me, and I'll work on world peace

Always lending a helping hand

A Meeting With My Mind

Before you assist all these other countries

Can you guys take care of our land?

You are selling our country city by city

And the economy soars higher and higher

You were voted not because you were the best man

But maybe the best liar

If you would have done half the things you promised

Then we'd be in a better place

You hold the highest job in the land

But to some Americans, you are a disgrace

The media keeps us informed on your whereabouts

And all the high-powered people you'll meet

While you wine and dine and wave at us on t.v.

The homeless continue to sleep on the streets.

You said, in the primaries, you would show concern

For all U.S. taxpayers

But like all the rest of your counterparts

You swore if elected, you'd be big tax slayers

4 years into your term, what happened?

To all the promises you made

I try to keep my head up

But all your promises seem to fade

You promised to touch up the welfare system

And bring thousands of new jobs

Still, unemployment is at an all-time high

And you wonder why people steal and rob

You promised to go after all the refineries

That's polluting our air

One lie after another

Political leaders, do you really think that's fair?

You promised if elected

Children's education would be priority

With all the different nationalities in the world

Any race could be a minority

I promise if I'm elected

I'll do like all those elected officials before me

And make sure the U.S. stays neglected

Scandals after scandals, that's all we hear

But I'm not trying to create a big fuss

We can't trust you. We sure can't believe you

So, whom can we really trust?

A Meeting With My Mind

THE AMERICAN DREAM

We live our lives with hopes of achieving the American dream

Some people have literally worked themselves to death

Society says the American dream is the ultimate goal in life

Millions of people have chased the American dream

Right down to their very last breath

I'm saying many have died trying to reach this goal

Society knows this is not an easy thing to do

Yet, society, you swear if we work real hard

Just like that, the American dream will come true

So, society, many have followed your plan to fulfill their dream

Working hard 7 days a week around the clock

Tired, weary bodies broken down mentally and physically

Our goal is the American dream; therefore, we cannot stop

Society, what is your definition of the American dream?

I heard, it's having a good job, nice car, and a house on the hill

But millions have died trying to attain these goals

So, tell me, society, how does that make you feel?

Does that make you a mass murderer or a serial killer?

Society, will you ever step up and take the blame?

Can we, the people, accuse you of genocide?

With all the lives lost, society, do you feel any guilt or shame?

Let's say we achieve the American dream you set for us

Society, where do we go from there?

Damn, why am I asking you that question?

People dying every day in the name of the American dream

So, it's pretty obvious you don't really care

If you did, you would make the American dream more realistic

Society, I challenge you to practice what you preach

People have worked hard for 30, 40, 50 years on their jobs

And the American dream is still out of reach

So, as I continue to do my part to achieve the American dream

I'll continue to work hard to my very last breath

I'll live the rest of my life chasing the American dream

Probably until I work myself to death

A Meeting With My Mind

POETICALLY THINKING

I closed my eyes but couldn't sleep. I tossed and turned all night
Woke up, dropped to the floor with a pen and pad. I began to write.

I wrote about the good times; I wrote about the bad times too
Basically, I was just poetically speaking poetically from me to you

My mind is so discombobulated. I guess I got so much to tell
There are many people worse off than me, so I guess all is well

My mind is just spinning to the thought of winning. Tell me you understand
I'm sure I'm not the only person thinking of a master plan

When times are rough, I keep my head up, never looking toward the ground
I set my goals high as the sky because that's where goals can be found

Who says I can't be a doctor or lawyer? What the hell, even the president
And why can't Hollywood or Beverly Hills be my residence

Who says a Lexus, Benz, or Rolls Royce can't be my luxury car
And why can't I have my own personal jet when I need to travel far

Can you see me sailing around the world on an ocean liner cruise?

Or be a famous poet like Maya Angelou or even Langston Hughes

I can be another Martin Luther King Jr. and bring peace all by myself

With hard work and determination, I, too, can have a Nobel Peace Prize on my shelf

I'm trying to say you can be anything in life if you set your mind to it

Make your goals in life your master plan, and let no one say you can't do it

I NEED TO GET OUT OF THE GHETTO

I need to get out of the ghetto

I'm running out of time

I need to get out quick

Before I become another victim of a violent crime

I need to get out of the ghetto

It's simply no more fun

Every time I leave my house

I wonder, do I need to take my gun

I need to get out of the ghetto

It's rough if you have no pull

A Meeting With My Mind

The police are having a standoff

With the gangbangers and pit bulls

I need to get out of the ghetto

The dope dealers are looking for new buyers

Compared to surrounding cities

Our grocery store prices are always higher

I need to get out of the ghetto

I feel I'm running out of patience

I can't even pump my own gas

The dope addicts are at every station

I need to get out of the ghetto

I fear going to McDonald's for a Big Mac

I'm afraid I might get held up

Or be a victim of a carjack

I need to get out of the ghetto

They say you're either hard or you're soft

I need to get my car repaired

9 times out of 10, I'll get ripped off

I need to get out of the ghetto

A Meeting With My Mind

There's definitely a lack of jobs
Who's to blame for all the people
Who chooses to steal and rob

I need to get out of the ghetto
The few jobs that are available just don't pay
The gangs have taken over the parks
My kids have nowhere to play

I need to get out of the ghetto
On just about any corner, you can buy drugs
The same little kids I grew up with
Are now the neighborhood thugs

I need to get out of the ghetto
I feel one day, I may have to kill
Forgive me, God, for talking like that
Only you know the pain I feel

I need to get out of the ghetto
I dream of living in a bit new house
Instead, I'm setting traps every night
Trying to catch the big rat or mouse
I need to get out of the ghetto

I just want to live by the "Golden Rules."
I can't get mad at my kids
If they're not learning in a ghetto school

I need to get out of the ghetto
I can't live off a welfare donation
I really just want my kids to have an opportunity
For a decent education

I need to get out of the ghetto
It just makes me feel very poor
I wish I could see a school on every corner
Instead of a liquor store

I need to get out of the ghetto
I'm tired of seeing gang fights
On my street to hide when it gets dark
They shoot out the streetlights

I need to get out of the ghetto
No more low-riders and their hopping cars
Every house on my block is protected
By heavy iron burglar bars

A Meeting With My Mind

I need to get out of the ghetto

I never know what might happen next

I'm not surprised if I see a hooker and a "John"

In the car, having sex

I need to get out of the ghetto

I just want to inhale fresh air

I want to go somewhere, anywhere

Where I know my family will be treated fair

I need to get out of the ghetto

I'm sick of all the cigarettes and beer

I watch my back daily

But still, I live every day in fear

I need to get out of the ghetto

Honestly, I think I'm losing my mind

Peace, love, and happiness

Is all I'm trying to find

I need to get out of the ghetto

It just makes me want to scream and shout

Plain and simple, no if, and, or buts

I just need to get out

MINIMUM WAGE

I'm tired of working all day, and my pay is minimum wage

Would I be wrong if I went to work and just went into a rage?

40 long hard hours, and my pay is 170 dollars

After Uncle Sam takes his, I can't help but scream and holler

Yeah, I got dreams of owning a big house on top of the hill

Congress, you got it made, so I guess you will never know how it feels

Working hard all-day flipping burgers, knowing I'm only getting $4.25

Congress, do you ever take time to think about how a person can survive?

How can I buy clothes for myself, let alone feed my kids?

Boss always looking over my shoulder, trying to find the tips I hid

It's 1996, and minimum wage is a disgrace

$4.25 an hour of hard labor and sweat pouring down my face

The owner keeps telling me don't worry; one day, I'll get a raise

I'll be making more money because then I'll be working 7 days

Then I'll be able to buy me some new socks to put on my aching feet

He says I'll be dipping french fries, no more flipping hamburger meat

I'll get plenty of overtime and make two dollars more

That will change my minimum wage, but damn, I'll still be poor

I guess congress never heard of a "cost of living" increase

They cut the money pie in half, and $4.25 is still my piece

I guess congress also never heard of the word we call inflation

I'll probably make more money panhandling and asking for donations

But soon, and very soon, I'll be able to turn the page

I'll move up to the cash register no more minimum wages

POWERLESS

The President has power to veto

The Congress can pass a bill

The Senate can raise our taxes

The military can legally kill

The D.A. can prosecute you.

The police can put you in jail

The judge can sentence you to life

The bondsman can let you post bail

The social worker can give you food stamps

The county can put you on welfare

The Salvation Army can give you shelter

The state pays for the poor's Medicare

The DMV can issue you a driver's license

The traffic judge can take them away
The IRS can keep your income tax check
And give you a bill you still must pay

The professor can teach you knowledge
The employer can give you a raise
The preacher says he can heal you
The mafia says crime pays

The lawyer can get you a plea bargain
The doctor can change a boy to a girl
But all these people with all this power
Can't bring peace and love to this world
I'm just a nobody in this cold, cruel world
I'm just a nobody in this cold, cruel world
Nobody ever listens to what I have to say
So to all you people with all this power
Make a change, unite, join hands, kneel, and pray

A Meeting With My Mind

THE MARCH OF A MILLION

History was made on October 16, 1995

A million Black men came together trying to keep hope alive

Critics said it was stupid. Others said it was a waste of time

A million Black men standing together made on powerful mind

They came to keep the dream alive, striving to reach the mountain top

A million Black men together tell me how they could be stopped

They marched on the nation's capital; fists held high to show unity

Vowing to themselves and the world to bring love back to their communities

Many didn't believe it could happen how Blacks could have that kind of power

A million Black men together now that's the "shock of the hour."

They marched because they wanted to make one man's dream come true

A million Black men together representing me and you

There were tears of sorrow and joy many thought that was kind of odd

A million Black men came together in 1995, each a child of God

I've never seen that many Black men together; man, what a beautiful sight

A million Black men holding hands, now that was alright

They came from all around the world; it was truly a show of love

A million Black men together with help from the man above

Let's not forget the old saying, "together we stand, divided we fall."

A million Black men came together now that should say it all

How could the messenger be so dark and the message he delivered be so bright?

A million Black men reaching the end of the tunnel where there was the light

So, as we go on in this lifetime, let's not forget October 16, 1995

A million Black men marching together just trying to keep our hopes alive.

CHAPTER ELEVEN
400 YEARS OF TEARS

SICK AND TIRED

I'm sick and tired of being sick and tired
I've been sick of being sick and tired way too long
Feels like the weight of the universe is upon my shoulders
I'm truly sorry, but I'm just not that strong
I've tried everything I could to make life better
No matter how hard I've tried, I just can't seem to win
I guess I can say I've been dealt a bad hand in this lifetime
Like a bad poker deal, I'm ready to toss this hand in

I've done some good deeds in this lifetime.
I guess the bad things I've done outweigh the good
If I could relive my life, would I make any changes?
I must admit yes, God knows surely would
I think it might be the color of my skin
I've had my fair share of being disrespected
I had a few opportunities to succeed in this lifetime
For some reason, those opportunities were usually neglected

I've always said, "thank you, yes, mama, and yes, sir."
My parents taught me that was the right thing to do
Besides, I've never disrespected "Old Glory."
Or should I say the red, white, and blue

A Meeting With My Mind

One day my life will be over in this lifetime

Luckily, I've come to the realization

That in this lifetime, I was just a pea in the pod

Therefore, no one owes me any explanations

PIECE OF THE PIE

Been on this Underground Railroad for 200 years
It's 2009, and I finally made it back
I see isn't much changed since I've been gone
Society still calling us "Black."

White man sleeping with one eye open
Got his finger on the trigger
I heard we got us a Black president of the United States of America
But society still calling us niggers

I thought by now, things would have changed
Is this modern-day slavery?
Just like it was 200 years ago
We still searching for justice and equality

We been fighting for our rights for 200 years.
All we want is freedom and equal rights before we die
Oh yeah, society, one more thing
A tiny slice of the American pie

LOOKING BACK

Looking back on my Black history

How did we survive all the misery?

I ask myself this again and again

Still, hard times since way back then

We've given our blood, sweat, and tears

Monumental loss of so many, so dear

Shackled by necks, legs locked with chains

Hatred, instead of blood running through our veins

Picking cotton from sunup to sundown

Upon our faces, a permanent frown

Dead ancestors floating down the river Nile

Never, ever a reason to smile

Raped my slave ancestors not a day in jail

Slave masters, I hope you burn in hell

The "Door of no Return" boarded slave ships

Try to rebel 10 lashes with the whip

Unthinkable pain to young and old

Upon auction blocks, my poor ancestors sold

Branded with hot iron through skin coats

Hung from nooses around their throats

Nowhere to hide, nowhere to run

A Meeting With My Mind

Try to escape dying by master's gun

Still never first, always last

Damn, I hate to think about the past

400 years is way too long

Still suffering, but we remain strong

IF I COULD TURN BACK THE HANDS ON THE CLOCK

What would I do if I could turn back the hands on the clock?

I would go back so far in time there would never have been auction blocks

There would never have been a time in history known as slavery

I would go back and congratulate all the slaves who still showed bravery

I would go back so far there would never have been slave ships

I would beat the hell out of those so-called "Masters" with their own ships

I would go back and reward all the slaves with pensions and back pay

And for every day my people suffered, I would make every day a holiday

I would go back and make a master key to unlock the shackles on their feet

I'd take that hot iron and brand them Masters like U.S.D.A. spoiled meat

I would throw life jackets to all the slaves thrown overboard

A Meeting With My Mind

I would be the lead singer as we all sang hymns to the song "Precious Lord."

I would untie all the nooses from the necks of the slaves hung from trees

I'd turn my head on those so-called "Masters" as they beg on bended knees

I'd make sure there were justice, freedom, and equality for me as well as you

I'd lethally inject all those masters who felt slavery was the right thing to do

I thank God for all the freedom fighters; one day, we'll be free at last

Man, I just wish it was a way I could erase some of the past

Think about all our ancestors who were raped by the masters out of lust

And all the poor people who were forced to ride in the back of the bus

I'd go back and put the shoe on the other foot, put their race in our place

And laugh my head off when I see the expression on the master's face

Let's say if Black's were the Masters and whites were slaves back then, and hatred was not a sin

And they were punished not for what they did wrong but only for the color of their skin

Would they forgive us, or would they think slavery was right?

What if we assassinated all the Presidents for not fighting for equal rights?

I thank God for the strength given to us as we continue to struggle and fight.

If I could turn back the hands on the clock, there'd be no Black or white.

HERE I STAND

Here I stand, gun in hand

Barrel in my mouth

No crisis negotiator needed

This is the way I choose to go out

Tired of being treated like a 5th class citizen

My whole life being classified as "Nigger"

The emotional scars I'm left to live with

Have driven me to place my finger on this trigger

Lord, forgive me for all my sins

As I drop down to my knees

Soon, they won't be able to call me "Nigger" again

With something as slight as a squeeze

The color of my skin has been a lifetime sin

So, I'll end with a single bullet

One-shot to the head, POW, now the body is dead

My finger is already on the trigger, so I pull it

A Meeting With My Mind

In the blink of an eye and one last sigh

My dead body hits the ground

With all the madness going on in the world today

I'm finally at peace, and I don't hear a sound

ALL ABOARD

Took me a trip aboard a slave ship

Some 400 hundred years ago

This ship didn't have any sleeping cabins

We all slept on the ship's floor

Chained by wrist and ankles

Heavy steel shackles locked around my neck

Crammed up two by twos, 700 strong

While the master's stayed on the top deck

Blood, sweat, and tears running down my face

My nigga sisters and babies all crying on one accord

And when they wouldn't shut up fast enough

The slave masters tossed them overboard

After all we done for them slave masters

How could the slave masters do that to them?

A Meeting With My Mind

They sho' nuff gonna die right away

Because none of us know how to swim

The tides are high, and the sea is rough

We chained up, so what can we do

Slave master won't tell us where this ship is going

They won't even give us a clue

No windows to look out, no fresh air to breath

Them slave masters don't know how cold it is down here

We been sailing weeks, and the odor is unbearable

You could actually smell the fear

I'm trying to keep these ladies from crying

They too small to know what's going on

I could hear my peoples on the upper deck

Humming them old gospel songs

I've never sailed on any slave ship before

I thought it was going to be fun

Slave masters getting joy out of popping us with them whips

Knowing we don't have nowhere to run

Open flesh wounds on all my slave brothers and sisters

Tears of pain running down their face

Slave masters feeding us bread and water

We done forgot how real food taste

My rib cage showing through my skin

We starving to death because we have not ate

A Meeting With My Mind

And those who passed away on this cruel journey

Slave masters using those dead bodies for shark bait

We been some good house and field niggas

Keeping masters' plantations and mansions clean

So, why, please God, tell me why?

These slave masters could be so mean.

Master yelled down to us, "y'all niggas not worth nothing."

They say we got 2 more weeks before we dock

Master said all of us that got any strength left

We going to be the first ones on the auction block

Please, God, sink this slave ship and bring us all home

And when the slave ship docks, and master opens the ship doors

Let us all be gone

Wouldn't that be nice

CHAPTER TWELVE
SUNSHINE AND RAIN

RAIN

Rain, rain, go away

I want to go outside so I can play

I did my homework

Now, it's time for fun

I want to ride my bike, skate, jump rope, and run

I want to yell, make noise, and just be free

So rain, rain, please go away for me

A Meeting With My Mind

AT THE END OF THE RAINBOW

At the end of the rainbow, there's a pot of gold

At the end of the rainbow is where I want to be

I've heard about this pot of gold since I was a kid

This pot of gold is something I would like to see

I don't know exactly where the rainbow starts

I have no idea where the rainbow ends

I want to find that pot of gold real bad

So, I can tell all my family and friends

Maybe I'll start from the middle of the rainbow

And make my way to the right

I'll drive and walk and drive and walk

All-day and all through the night

I'll search over every mountain top

I'll even sail the seven seas

I'll turn over every unturned rock

I'll look behind all the big redwood trees

The rainbow can be seen for many miles

Maybe I'll turn back and go the other way

I really want to see this pot of gold so bad

I won't stop looking until my last living day

Suddenly from afar, I see a bright shining light

Which tells me the pot of gold is very near

As I jump, shout, and scream with joy

The beautiful rainbow suddenly disappears

A GENTLE GIANTS PLEA

My world down here is beautiful

The water is very clear

Helicopters, sirens, and gunshots

Is something I never hear

I mind my own business in the underworld

I'm as humble as can be

I don't try to hurt mankind

So, why do they hunt to kill me

Thousands of my friends have been caught and slaughtered

Some of us have been trained to behave

I remember when we all used to play together

Jumping out of the water, splashing on the waves

Mankind has the wrong perception of me

They just don't seem to realize

A Meeting With My Mind

I get along with everybody down here

I'm a whale, and I'm supposed to be big for my size

The scenery is beautiful down below

Scenery like you've never seen before

You might see a pool of us swim by

And wave our fins at you ashore

It used to be really crowded down here

But thanks to mankind, a lot of us are now gone

So, for those of us still living in the underworld

Mankind, please just leave us alone

TODAY IS THE DAY

Today is the day that the Lord has made

So, tell me what you are gonna do

If you believe this, I mean no disrespect

But this poem may not be suitable for you

It's for all the non-believers in the world

Those who don't believe the Lord has made this day

For it was the Lord who blew the breath of life in you

It was the Lord who started you on your way

It was he who helped you out of bed

It was the Lord who said, ask in his name

Please don't quote me, but that's what the Lord said

It was he who made the sun rise this morning

And when night falls, he'll present us with the moon

For today is the day that the Lord has made

Prepare yourself because it's said he'll be back real soon

It was he who held the guiding light in the tunnel

It was the Lord who helped you make it to the other end

For today is the day the Lord has made

I suggest you go out and tell a friend

It was he who helped you down the path of righteousness

When in reality, you thought you were lost

A Meeting With My Mind

The Lord's love is unconditional

And the best part of all

His love is free, and it comes at no cost

It was he who told you not to give up today

The race of life is hard, believe in him, and you can win it

For today is the day that the Lord has made

Let us all rejoice and be glad in it

BUTTERFLY

Please let me introduce myself; they call me "butterfly."

I come in many shapes and beautiful colors, but it's only a disguise

I'm born as a caterpillar and transformed into such a beautiful thing

With a small body, a pair of antennas, and a set of beautiful wings

I'm one of God's most unique creations, and I'm as humble as can be

I'm loved throughout the world; people have such a passion for me

Like dogs are to man, flowers are considered by best friend

Wherever flowers blossom upon them, I descend

People chase me all around trying to catch me, but it's all in fun

To harm anyone in any way is something I've never done

I AM A FLOWER

I'm the most beautiful gift given in the world one could ever bring

I'm a beautiful creation from God, and I blossom every spring

I come in white, purple, yellow, pink, blue, and even red

One sniff of my lovely scent and I'm sure to cloud your head

They say I look beautiful on your clothes; people wear me in their hair

People give me away by the dozens; that's fine with me. I don't care

To some, I'm said to bring more joy and smiles than a pot of gold

Well, ok, they say I mean just as much, at least that's what I've been told

Every year I must admit to you, I look forward to those April showers

That produces me by the millions, for I am a flower

A Meeting With My Mind

M-E-O-W

Let me tell you something about us

That might help you understand

We are considered lady's best friend

Just like dogs are to man

We make adorable pets. We are furry

And loved so much

We're fuzzy and huggable

I wouldn't trade my cat for anything

Sometimes it's good, sometimes it's bad

I've lost many friends to a hit-and-run driver

Which to me is very sad

We don't hurt anybody, we don't cause trouble

All we want to do is have a little fun

But when we're being chased by a big dog

Boy, we sure can run

We don't chase bones, fetch frisbees

But we are very smart

We can find food when we're hungry

And we know how to get to your heart

The myth in this society is

Black cats only bring bad luck

I bet you won't find us riding

On the hood of no fire truck

We don't bark all night and day

We give our owners lots of rest

We're not trying to brag or nothing

But as pets, we are best

MR. OCEAN

Sitting on the dock of the bay, staring at the blue sea

I came here to tell you, Mr. Ocean, you're not what you used to be

Millions have sailed your water, and by sailors, you've been saluted

I remember when you were so clean and clear. Now you're so polluted

I used to come here to swim, and in my mouth, you would leave a salty taste

Now I'm scared to touch you because you're filled with chemical waste

Some come to spread the ashes of loved ones, some come to make a wish

Many come to fetch their dinner, but the signs say, "Don't eat the fish."

People use you for their vacation; you offer them lots of pleasure

Divers explore your depths in search of lots of treasure

You're calm when you want to be, but sometimes you can be very mean

Mr. Ocean, there are people who care about you and try to keep you clean

With tears in my eyes, sitting at the bay, staring at the filthy sea

I hate to admit it, Mr. Ocean, you're just now what you used to be

A Meeting With My Mind

NATURE CALL

I come here to think and just to get away

I come here to relax after I've had a rough day

I come here to get a whiff of nature's fresh air

I come here for the view no other can compare

I come here because there is no smog, no air pollution

I come here to contemplate my thoughts when I need a solution

I come here to get naked, lay back, and enjoy the breeze

I come here to hear the birds sing as they hide in nature's trees

I come here to enjoy nature, being so calm, cool, and collective

I come here to try and put my life in its' proper perspective

I come here to imagine what it's like standing on the mountain top

I come here because the weather is never too cold or too hot

I come here to look at myself in the water because it's so clear

I come here to let my guards down; out here, I have no fears

A Meeting With My Mind

I come here to release all the stress that is clogging up my mind

I come here to walk your paths, never knowing what I might find

I come here to seek new heights and simply reach for the sky

I come here to express my emotions when I want to cry

I come here to enjoy nature and just to be alone.

I come here because I love nature; this is my home away from home.

ROSE

R is for the pretty RED color you show

O is for your OUTSTANDING beauty we all know

S is for your lovely fragrance SMELL

E is for the EFFECTS you bring; we all know so well.

SHORELINES OF HAWAII

I strolled the shorelines of a beautiful Hawaiian beach

Letting the crystal-clear waters run through my bare feet

Hand in hand with my lovely lady

While listening to some slow jam beat

I strolled the shorelines of a beautiful Hawaiian beach

As the night stars sparkled in her eyes

We kissed and made love under the "cherry moon."

That lit up the nighttime sky

I strolled the shorelines of a beautiful Hawaiian beach

Dreaming that I was in paradise

Even though I'm many, many miles away

The thought of being there just seems so nice

SURFING

All I want to do is surf, just me against the ocean's waves

Party on the beach with some friends and watch the beautiful babes

I want to surf the water tunnels until the waves break

Afterward, lounge under a palm tree and watch some buttocks shake

I'll even take a few wipeouts as I try to master the famous "hang ten."

And tomorrow, as the sun rises, be there to do it all again

I'll attack the waves with nothing but a surfboard in my hand

And when I'm finished for the day, I'll make castles out of sand

I love to surf the waters until the setting of the evening sun

I just want to surf, and surf, and surf, and surf

To me, surfing is just so much fun

CHAPTER THIRTEEN
THE POET

DO CALL ME A POET

Do call me a poet if that's who you really feel

I've never written non-fiction; I only write what's real

Do call me poet if what I write you feel is true

Read any poem I've written, and within it, you'll find you

Do call me a poet if you believe in what I say

I'll share society's pain and sorrow in my own special way

Do call me a poet if what I write has made you cry

I only write from within my heart; my heart won't tell a lie

Do call me a poet if I have mended a broken heart

For I am only one in a million, but one is still a part

Do call me a poet if I have helped you make a right decision

I guarantee you'll find relief if you read my poems on religion

Do call me a poet if I've guided you in the right direction

Those that read my first book know I, too, need love and affection

Do call me a poet if my poems have helped you deal with grief

I'm very sentimental to your needs, pain I try to relieve

Do call me a poet if that's what you think of me

A poet is how I want to be remembered, so a poet is what I shall be

A Meeting With My Mind

I HEARD THE POET EXPRESS LIFE WITH HIS PEN

I heard the Poet, and now I seem to know it

I know he wants us to look at life for what it is

It brings us sunshine; it brings us rain

It brings us joy, and it brings us pain

In spite of what it brings, he wants us to be encouraged to continually sing.

Sing songs of joy, love, and eternal praise

God created us for this purpose, that our hearts, souls, and minds would be raised.

Raised to a place of knowledge, understanding, and inspiration

To rise up from our places of despair, hopelessness, and frustration

The Reverend Jesse Jackson told us to keep hope alive

And I know that the Poet wants nothing less than for us to continue to strive

Strive towards the audacity to hope as our great President Obama recommends

A recommendation to hope in your future, hope in God, hope in your dreams and hope to set original trends.

Be an original, the work of art that God created you to be

Be all that you can be, and in the process, you will begin to see

To see the world as the Poet sees it.

A world full of broken people who are still under construction

God is the construction worker behind the scenes, and he will fix it as he designed it to function

Therefore, don't give up, and no matter what it looks like, don't give in

The Poet merely confronted life for what is and has been

Through the words expressed with his pen

THEY DIDN'T KNOW

They call me a product of the ghetto

They say the ghetto is where I live

But they dare to make a change

Assistance they refuse to give

They say I'll never be anything

They won't even give me a chance

It's funny they really don't understand

Knowledge, I continue to enhance

They say I'll never be productive

I'll never hold a decent job

Malcolm X said, "by any means necessary."

Be it cheat, steal, or rob

They say I'll always be second class

They tell me I'll never reach the mountain top

Dr. Martin Luther King made it

Therefore, I refuse to stop

They call me a bastard child

My pops left me because he was hooked on dope

What they didn't know is God has always been on my side

And with God, there is always hope

I'D PROBABLY WRITE ABOUT

If I wrote a poem every day of the year

I would probably have to write no more

I would cover everything from A to Z

I would write about the rich and the poor

I'm sure I'd write about the war that's going on

And all the innocent soldiers dying

I'd definitely write about our political leaders

You know, the ones who are always lying

I'd write about the evil parents

Committing horrible crimes against their own kids

I'd write about the 3-strike law

That's putting people away for 25-year prison bids

I'd write about the thousands of homeless people

Living under freeway bridges and sleeping on the streets

I'd write about world hunger for sure

People dying because they have no food to eat

I'd write about illegal immigration

Running rampant in the U.S.A.

I'd write about drugs and street thugs

Kids having nowhere safe to play

How could I not write about catholic priests?

A Meeting With My Mind

Those who have committed such ungodly sins

Preying on and molesting young altar boys

All the time pretending to be their friends

I'd probably write about global warming

Being blamed for the earth's ozone pollution

Or I'd probably just write one long poem

Asking the world, can we find some solutions?

THE MIRROR

I looked in the mirror to bring out my inner thoughts

But really, I was just joking

The mirror looked right back at me

And suddenly, the mirror became broken

Indeed, it shed some light on me

It also shaded the dark

The flame of life that once burned inside of me

Is now nothing other than a spark

I talked to the mirror, and it politely spoke right now

What it said, I could not hear

I thought to myself, how could that be

When upon the mirror I'm standing so near

The mirror brought back memories of the past

Some memories I'd rather leave behind

When I look in the mirror, it stares right back at me

So, I know the mirror is not blind

I ask the mirror to forgive me

For anything I've done wrong in the past

I can't run from this mirror, for it is gloomy

The reflection looks like that of overcast

I've come to you looking my best

For mirror, you have even seen me cry

I've made so many broken promises to you

That I can't even deny

Sometimes I can't even face you, mirror

I refuse to look you eye to eye

You seem to know when I'm telling the truth

And you definitely know when I'm telling a lie

Sometimes the mirror becomes very foggy

I wipe you off to see you clear

I can fool some people some of the time

But I have yet to fool the mirror

I scratch my head time after time

And ask myself, how can that be?

If I try to fool the reflection in the mirror

Who would I really be fooling nobody but me?

JUST WISHING

I watched the sunrise this morning

I watched darkness turn to light

I thanked God for another breath of life

Hoping today everything will be alright

Many things will happen in the world today

Some good things and, of course, some bad

Hopefully, for me, everything good will happen

Because the bad days, enough of them I've had

I wish the best for my family

Wishing we all live to see another day

I wish the same thing for the entire world

From sea to shining sea

I wish for love and unity throughout my community

Oh God, how I wish this is how the world could be

If I could, I'd stop the wars that are going on

With the stroke of a pen, I'd bring all wars to an end

I wish I could line up all the soldiers in every country

Have them all shake hands and be friends

Imagine a day with no one dying

Be it murder, sickness, or of natural cause

I wish we could all live just one day in this lifetime

Where everyone would respect and obey man's laws

My parents taught me to always love thy fellow man

If I should fall in your presence, please lend me a helping hand

Close your eyes for just a minute

Act as though you could not see

Make me a wish for the good of the world today

I wonder, will your wish include me?

WITHIN ME

I had a talk with the man upstairs today

I told him exactly what was on my mind

I explained to him joy, love, and happiness on earth

Is something I cannot find

I searched the highest mountain top

Hillsides and the valleys below

I looked to the east, west, north, and south

God guide me in the direction I should go

Take my hand and lead me, dear Lord

I walk with you every single day

I put all my trust in you, dear Lord

I can't imagine having it no other way

I know joy, love, and happiness has to be somewhere.

Dear Lord, tell me, oh, where could it be?

The Lord spoke to me and said, "Listen, son,

Joy, love, and happiness doesn't come in a physical form."

He said, "they can all be found right within me."

A Meeting With My Mind

THE BOOK OF TERRELL (VERSES ACCORDING TO ME)

I raise my hand to praise you, dear Lord

For giving me life, another day

If I had a choice to do it again tomorrow

I'm proud to say I wouldn't choose any other way

I give praises to you, dear Lord, throughout the day

Looking towards the heavens hoping you hear

It is you who makes it possible for me, dear Lord

To walk through the shadows of the valley of death

And I, too, have no fear

I talk to people every day, dear Lord.

Who still can't believe you gave your only begotten son

And whosoever believes in you shall not perish

But have everlasting life

Wow, now that's what I call fun

You see, my cup runs over for you, dear Lord

I'm constantly testifying how you anoint my soul

Many are afraid to praise your name, dear Lord

But I'm overjoyed to let the story be told

A Meeting With My Mind

I tell people the Lord is my shepherd. I shall not want

If you ask in his name, you shall receive

I'm constantly telling friends he could do the same for you

But first, in the Lord, they must believe

He may not come when you want him

But believe me, he's always on time

You can call the Lord long distance any hour of the day

And it won't even cost you a dime

I tell friends, "Ask in the Lord's name for anything

And believe me, it shall be given."

For it was the Lord who woke you today

To be among the land of the living

I tell people all the time, dear Lord

There's power when you pray

Who else can take a hurricane or thunderstorm?

And turn it into a bright sun shining day.

I tell people, Lord, you'll be there for them

When they think they don't have a friend

A Meeting With My Mind

The part that people don't believe the dearest Lord

Is when I tell them, "Ask, and he'll forgive you for all your sins."

So, as I bring this poem to an end, dear Lord

I walk by faith, not by sight

As long as I keep praising your holy name, dear Lord

I, myself, know everything will be alright

CHAPTER FOURTEEN

FREESTYLE

(ALL IN A DAY'S WORK)

A Meeting With My Mind

ALLOW ME TO INTRODUCE MYSELF

I come from a family of killers

Believe me, I'm as bad as I want to be

People have given their own lives

Just to hang out with me and my family

I have no remorse or respect for no one

People treat me like I'm their best friend

Yeah, I let them make a little money off me

Then, I reward them with 5, 10, or 15 years in the state or federal pen.

I have no conscious; I destroy whole families

Mothers, fathers, cousins, little boys, and girls

I'm more popular than any man in this universe

I wreak havoc throughout the world

I don't see what people see in me.

I'm ruthless. I even go after your fetus before birth

No monetary amount can scare me

I'll take a millionaire for all he's worth

The strongest have tried to go against me.

A Meeting With My Mind

I'm small in stature but a heavyweight champ pound for pound

One by one, they continue to challenge me

Check any cemetery and see how many I've put in the ground.

I've traveled with the most beautiful ladies in the world

In and out of every major airport

I travel first class, sometimes in a stash

Every now and then, you'll find me in court

People try to take advantage of me

So, I pay them back by putting them in jail

I'll make them lose their house, cars, job, and families

I'll make it impossible for you to post bail

Let me introduce my family, this weed, meth, heroin, and ecstasy

Our main objective is to seek and destroy the brains

Oh, excuse me, I'm sorry, I almost forgot to introduce myself

I'm the baby of the family; just call me cocaine.

A Meeting With My Mind

IF

If I could, I would. I should

We've all heard that saying before

If I live by God's commandments

Maybe I'll be let through heaven's door

If I didn't honor thy mother and father

Who knows where I would be

If it wasn't for my mother and father

There would definitely be no me

If I could make a rainbow last forever

Lord knows I truly would

If I could zap the world with a bolt of love

I'd do it today; please let that be understood

If I could erase racism with the stroke of a pen

How wonderful would this world be

If I could spread kindness, joy, love, and happiness

I'd make it last for eternity

If I could teach this world, we're all created equal

A Meeting With My Mind

Show society how to walk hand in hand
If I had the power to make this reality
With the help from the man above, I know I can

If I could stop all the wars of the world today
"Weapons of mass destruction" there would be no more
If I could stock all the shelves in the store with love
Then you could buy love right out of the store

If I could, I'd wave a magic wand
Put a beautiful smile on everyone's face
If I could, I'd break the magic wand when I'm done
So, those smiles could never be erased

If I could, I'd open the ears to all the deaf
I'd return the blind back their vision
If I could make this one wish come true
The whole world would live under one religion

If I could take the word "hunger" out of the dictionary
I'd make sure everyone in the world has food to eat
If I could, I'd do anything in my power
To get the homeless off society's streets

If I didn't have such strong faith in my heavenly father

Would the devil be my best friend?

If I should die before I wake, please contact Jesus

For he is my next of kin

LOVE

L is for LONGEVITY

That's what I want this relationship to be

O is for OUTSTANDING

That's what you truly are to me.

V is for VIOLET

My favorite color by far

E is for EVERLASTING

Our LOVE will shine like the brightest star.

A Meeting With My Mind

MY BEDTIME PRAYER

My heavenly Father blesses me as I kneel down and pray

Hear my bedtime prayer and thank you for life for another day

Bless my momma; I love her and my daddy too

God, when I grow up, I want to be just like you

Bless my sisters and brothers, my dog, and my cat

Bless my granny and grandpa and his old Dodger hat

Bless my uncles and aunties and my cousins galore

Bless McDonald's, Chuck E. Cheese, and all the candy stores

Bless my teachers, babysitter, and all my friends at school

Bless my pet hamster named Nemo; he's really super cool

Bless all the homeless people, man, woman, boy, and girl

I end my bedtime prayer by saying God bless the entire world.

MY HEART BEATS FOR YOU

My heart beats for you 100 m.p.h.

You're always on my mind.

I'm going to write this short poem for you

And try my best to make it rhyme

When the ink from my pen touches this paper

A Meeting With My Mind

A burning sensation begins inside of me

No matter what I'm doing at that minute

Or wherever I may happen to be

Just the thought of you brings chills to my body

And it happens like that all the time

This poem is short but strong in meaning

And I actually made it rhyme

NOT SO WISE

Sometimes I cry and don't know why

These tears roll down my face

I know somewhere, way out there

There has to be a better place

This place called earth, for what it's worth

Is a place I so despise

Ignorance has ruined society today

By those who consider themselves so wise

Look at our present situation today

Now you tell me who's to blame

The government is handing out I.O.U.'s

Yes, the powers to be, show no shame

Why are the elderly being abused so much?

We have war veterans sleeping on the street

People losing their homes daily

The homeless dumpster diving for food to eat

Schools closing down, college fees sky high

The decision-makers say to hell with higher education

Millions don't have medical insurance today

And soon, there'll be no more welfare donations

Corporate companies closing, space division barely holding

Can't believe banks are running out of money

We have priests and evangelists going to jail on the regular

You may laugh, but that's not funny

That just shows you the terrible times we're living in

Our elected officials are so damn corrupt

They claim to be wise, but all they do is lie

That's why so many people just don't give a fuck

Why should we care when our officials aren't fair?

We suffer daily from their bad decisions

People pray every day; on bended knees, we stay

Our only hope is what we believe in, our religion

Not trying to fuss, but if Uncle Sam cares about us

They wouldn't choose to make life so hard

Millions of dollars have been missing, managed by those so wise

But when it comes to us, it's total disregard.

PEN FATIGUE

I grabbed my pen and began to write, but upon my paper, there's no ink

I took my hat off and scratched my head, and suddenly I began to think

I shook my pen up and down, side to side, and again I try to write

A Meeting With My Mind

I pushed down hard, and still no ink; I'm pushing down with my entire might

So, I'm mind-boggled now trying to figure out is my mind playing tricks on me?

I really don't understand what's going on because my pen is my best friend, you see

Suddenly my pen jumps up and begins to write; I mean, it's writing all by itself.

The pen writes he's tired of writing about the bad times, and he's in bad pen health.

He says he's tired of writing about all the hatred, evil doings, trials, and tribulations.

He says he's tired of writing about this cruel world and all the racial discrimination.

He says he's tired of writing about the Emancipation Proclamation having a bad day.

He's tired of writing about the poor kids who are not safe when they go outside to play.

He says he's tired of writing about the good, bad, the happy, the sad. Life's ups and downs.

He says he's tired of writing about the late, great Black heroes; most are no longer around.

He says he's tired of writing about self-destruction, corruption, and long prison terms.

He says he's tired of writing about judges, athletes, and the big salaries they earn

He says he's tired of writing about exploitation, race segregation, and human rights.

A Meeting With My Mind

He says he's tired of writing about doctors giving abortions in the middle of the night.

He says he's tired of writing about small things, bling-bling, and the violence in the street.

He says he's tired of writing about poor people on skid row who have no food to eat.

He says he's tired of writing about the sun, the moon, and the beautiful stars.

He says he's tired of writing about the rich, the famous, and all their big fancy cars.

He says he's tired of writing about same-sex marriages, gays, homosexuals, and lesbians.

You must understand this is not me, the writer talking; these are words from my pen.

He says he's tired of writing about life in general, sex, drugs, and rock and roll.

He says he's tired of writing about pervert teachers and preachers; I need to rest my soul.

So as your pen, I guess you can say I'm laid off, I quit, I resign, or even I'm fired.

Keeping it real, I hope you understand how I feel. Plain and simple, I'm just pen tired.

PLEASE DO COME IN

I've finally found the woman of my dreams

I no longer need to look

I can now put the final period to end this chapter

I'm finally finished with my book

I can copyright this book now

I've finally found the right woman for me

One who says she'll accept me for who I am

And help me be the person I want to be

No more looking for her high and low

I only ask myself, after all these years, where have you been

I've finally found the woman of my dreams

My heart is wide open; please do walk right in

RIE

R – We all know roses are RED

Of course, this is so very true

RIE, God knows I'd be lost in this world

If I didn't have a beautiful woman like you

I – Is for INDESCRIBABLE, INTERTWINE

You and I twisted together like a rope

RIE, as long as I have you by my side

Tells me in my life, there's always hope

E – Is for EVERYTHING, EVERLASTING

RIE, the "E" means ETERNITY

There are no other words to describe my feelings

This is how I forever want our LOVE to be

MY ENDLESS LOVE

A Meeting With My Mind

SHE LEFT ME

My mother left me this morning

Left me, as in never to be seen again

Not only was she my mother, father, sister, brother

My mother was truly my best friend

God must have needed an angel up in heaven

Mother, you always said you wanted to go there

So, rather than let you endure the constant pain and suffering

God called you home to show you how much he cares

With all the kindness, joy, love, and happiness you shared while here

If I had to score your life, I'd give you a perfect 10

And when God reads your track record on judgment day

He'll tell the angels to personally let you in

God will read you were a schoolteacher for 30 years

That had to be a very hard thing to do

A schoolteacher isn't an occupation for everyone

I guess Mother, that's why God chose you

I thank you, dear Mother, for the abundance of love you gave

From out of your womb, you gave me life

Which makes it that much easier for me to understand

Why my father chose you as his lovely wife

Mother, you were my heart, soul, my reason for living

I wouldn't trade all the good times we shared for nothing in the world

No monetary amount could replace your values

Not even a bag full of rubies, diamonds, or pearls

Mother, I'm going to miss all the good times we shared

That big pretty smile upon your big, beautiful face

If the whole world smiled at the exact same time, Mother

Your smile could never be matched or replaced

SIZE DOES MATTER

I saw a hummingbird the other day

His tiny wings flapping as fast as can be

I stared at the bird in awe or disbelief

The little hummingbird stared right back at me

I said, "Excuse me, little birdie, don't mind me,

I'm not trying to mess up your day."

I outweigh this little birdie by 300 pounds

But it was I that tip-toed away

A Meeting With My Mind

The little birdie turned to me with a mean stare

As if to show me his long pointed sharp nose

I turned and began to run as fast as I could

You know how the old story goes

The bigger they are, the harder they fall

Was the only thing that came to my mind

I ran behind a car and ducked for cover

Didn't want to get stuck in my big behind

Now here I am having a stand-off.

With a little birdie that was 10 times smaller than me

I yelled out to the little birdie, "I don't want any problems,

You can have that damn tree!"

WELL EXCUSE ME!

I woke up this morning to the sounds of birds singing

Chirping such a beautiful hymn

Opened my window and pulled back the curtains

As I begin to chirp along with them

I did my best to impersonate the little birdies

I guess my chirping wasn't music to their ears

Suddenly all the little birdies chirping suddenly stopped

And just like that, all the little birdies disappeared

WHAT DO THEY KNOW?

What do they know about sharing the same thoughts that you don't even have to live on the same continent to know just what I'm thinking? What do they know about you laughing, me laughing so hard that we can't breathe, and tears are coming down our faces? What do they know?

What do they know about not breathing because you can't breathe, so I can't breathe, so we can't breathe without each other? What do they know about me getting lost into you and you falling into me and us knotted together because we fit, oh so perfectly? What do they know?

What do they know about the love that we share, the pain that we share, the heartbreaks that we share, the dreams that we share that one day we will raise together? What do they know?

What do they know about the restless nights and dreamless nights, and nights that you can't leave, and I don't want you to leave, and we say, "fuck it," and let it be? What do they know about endless conversations and pointless gossip and you knowing what I know and I knowing what you know, but it's between us, so no one else has to know? What do they know?

What do they know about you?

What do they know about me?

What do they know about us?

A Meeting With My Mind

What do they know about you living for me, dying for you?

Nothing! It can't be phantom. What do they know, you ask? Everything they know that this could never be, and it's not reality, but they better let us be. They know without you, there's no me; without me, there's no you, and without us, they would be so empty.

What do they know?

What do they know?

I ask, what do they know?

WHAT CAN YOU DO

What can you do to make a change?

Tell me, what's wrong? Why are you looking at me so strange?

What can you do? I said is that such a big task?

I'll never know the answer to the question if I don't ask

What can you do to make this world a better place?

Can you love thy fellow man regardless of their race?

What can you do to show society you really care?

Are you willing to lend a helping hand to those crying out in despair?

What can you do to overcome all of your trials and tribulations?

What can you do to bring peace, love, and happiness to this earth?

Are you afraid to do the work diligently with your neighbor for better or worse?

What can you do to stop all the senseless killings?

Believe it or not, there's something you can do, but are you willing?

What can you do to save the life of that unborn child?

Yea, I know that's deep, but sit back and think about that for a while

What can you do to somehow make a change in society for the better?

Write it down, seal it, address it to yourself, and mail it as a certified letter.

Because only you know what you can do to make a change

FINALLY

Finally, finally, finally

We've reached the last poem for this book

I truly hope you enjoyed yourself

On this lyrical journey, we just took

I took you to the mountain tops

We traveled the valleys below

We visited some of the mean ghettos

A place where some of you may never go

I took you to a couple of wars our country had

We even talked to "Oh Glory," the flag

We visited the homeless on skid row

Poor people living out of boxes and paper bags

I met many people I didn't know before this journey

I made hundreds of new friends

I truly wish this journey could go on forever

But as you all know, all good things must come to an end.

CHAPTER FIFTEEN

MAY I R.I.P.

DESTINATION HEAVEN'S GATE

I need to ask God to forgive me

I know it's never too late

I'm on a serious mission in life

Destination: Heaven's Gate

I need to reach my destination bad

There are some stories I need to tell

Destination: Heaven's Gate

Because I've already been through hell

Hell, right here on earth

The myth is it's always on fire

Destination: Heaven's Gate

Yeah, that is my true desire

This is a cruel, cruel world.

There are very few people down here that care

Destination: Heaven's Gate

Where I know all is fair

When I was born, I had no idea

A Meeting With My Mind

Life would be so hard

Destination: Heaven's Gate

There'll be no need for a security guard

I can't imagine people in this world

Could really be so mean

Destination: Heaven's Gate

For the light, I have seen

This little light of mine

While on earth, I'm going to let it shine

Destination: Heaven's Gate

Admission I hope to gain

I've faced all my trials and tribulations

And victory shall be won

Destination: Heaven's Gate

Mission complete when I hear God say, "A job well done."

A Meeting With My Mind

SUICIDE

This poem is very touching. Sit back, relax, and take this ride

I'm going to get kind of emotional and write about suicide

He lost his wife, gave up on life, and now he has no pride

So, he feels the only way out is to commit suicide

She says she has nothing to live for. She says she'd be better off dead

I know that sounds crazy, but yeah, that's what she said

You tell me, "How could being dead be better off than enjoying life"?

She could have been some kids' mother or some man's beautiful wife

He got fired from his job for stealing, and now he's very depressed

He decides to commit suicide to relieve himself from all the stress

If only he had someone to talk to; the note says he even called the suicide hotline

The answering machine says, "Sorry, we close our doors at nine."

"I'm only 13 and already pregnant" is what she wrote on her suicide note

She chose to commit suicide by hanging herself by the throat

He sits in his car all along, holding a big gun to his head

Saying to himself, "This will be easy, bang! In one second, I'll be dead."

She locks herself in the bathroom and opens a jar of pills

An overdose is her choice of suicide; she wonders, can something that small kill?

His family has turned their backs on him; his friends think he's insane

A Meeting With My Mind

He says, "What the hell!" and commits suicide by stepping in front of a train

She had an abortion and can't stop crying; the baby's daddy says he doesn't care

So, she ties a plastic bag over her head to keep her brain from getting any air

He's the sole provider for his family, so why is he climbing that bridge?

He got hurt on his job and can't work now; he can no longer put food in his fridge.

She's a runaway child, running wild, hanging with the neighborhood street thugs.

Not knowing her suicide would be her first experience with drugs

He's only nine and already a problem child; He rams a knife through his own heart

He was born and labeled a "crack baby" he had problems from the very start

It's Christmas, and she's very depressed. She didn't get a single gift

She straps herself and her kids in her car and drives it over a cliff

He kisses his wife and grabs his coat, off to another late-night meeting

She locks the door and drinks some Drano because she heard he's been cheating

She's overweight and has health problems; it's hard to get around

Knowing she can't swim a lick, she jumps in the swimming pool and drowns

He took all his money to Las Vegas and placed a $20,000 dollar bet

He crapped out, so he put one bullet in the chamber and plays a game of Russian Roulette

Her house is in foreclosure, her car repoed, her bills she could no longer pay

She says suicide will cure everything, so she dashes across the freeway

He's a Vietnam vet who lost both legs; he says Uncle Sam isn't treating him fair

So he sets himself on fire when all he wanted was a new wheelchair

There are foster kids, both parents OD'd, she's 8, and he's 11

They ran away and committed suicide together, hoping to see their parents in heaven

The most common form of suicide is the one where you slit your wrist

Believe it or not, someway, somehow, you will be truly missed

People die every day of natural causes. Some even die from air pollution

If you're thinking about suicide, hold up, there are still many solutions!

These are just some examples of suicide that are used every day

Ladies and gentlemen, boys and girls, believe me, suicide is not the way

You make me feel like the world is on your back. You may feel like there is nothing you can do

I know the feeling, believe me, I've thought plenty of times about suicide too

I know life is full of ups and downs, and the struggle is hard to bear

Please, before you choose suicide, think about it. There are people who care.

A Meeting With My Mind

DRIVE-BY AGONY

Yeah, Mr. Big Stuff, now are you proud of what you did?

You took the life of a precious, innocent, and beautiful little kid

One who could have been a doctor, lawyer, or even the president

Thanks to a drive-by shooting, an early grave is where he or she is sent

The young one never seen it coming. They didn't stand a chance

They never got to experience life or attend their first Valentine's dance

Who are you to take God's precious gifts that he brought into this world?

Yesterday you killed a little boy today, a pretty little girl

2 years old, 3, 4, 5, 6, and even 7

Killed in a drive-by shooting, their young souls already sent to heaven

Most of them caught off guard while playing or just having fun.

Not knowing they would leave here today from the bullet of a gun

They were never given a chance to finish elementary or high school

How does that make you feel, Mr. Big Stuff, or should I say Mr. Big Fool?

You took their life in a drive-by shooting before it really ever began

Now, if you were a real man, you would turn yourself in

But no, you run and hide like the coward you really are

You killed an innocent kid who had dreams of becoming a movie star

You once were a kid too, but God spared your childhood life

You killed a future football star or some man's future wife

Did that make you feel like a big man when you decided to pull the trigger?

So, now in front of your so-called homeboys, you feel a little bigger

You did a drive-by for revenge, which is stupid, or just to get a thrill

But you'll be held accountable come judgment day

Because even God said thou shalt not kill.

A Meeting With My Mind

FOR MY OBITUARY

The sun rose this morning. A new day has begun.

I live each day of my life not knowing if it's the last one

I think about what I'm going to do today and what I did the day before

And pray to God I live through this one so I can plan many more

I really don't know what my plans will be or what this day has in store

I had these same thoughts yesterday, déjà vu, I've been here before

I pray for my family each morning, Moms, Pops, sisters, and brothers

Hoping we all live through this day and praying we all see another

Some live life two ways, in the fast lane or in the slow

If I should die today, it means it was my time to go

Some may be happy I'm gone; others will forever live in sorrow

Truly, I would like to live today and hope I see tomorrow

No one knows what tomorrow brings. Let me make it through this day

So I can go to work, make it home safe, and watch my children play

There are a million places I can think of where I'd rather be

None could make me happier than a day out with my family

Now it's getting dark, and the sun is going down

Another day has passed. I thank God I'm still around

As I lay down to sleep, I pray I wake, but I don't know what time or when

Hopefully, it's in the morning, and I'll have these same thoughts again

But if by chance, I don't wake to fall on my knees and pray

I know I lived my life to the fullest each and every day.

MAYBE

Maybe you came to say goodbye

Maybe you came because you needed to cry

Maybe you came to shed some tears

Maybe you came to overcome your fears

Maybe you came from one last look

Maybe you came to sign the guest book

Maybe you came to bring a flower basket

Maybe you came just to see the casket

Maybe you came from way across town

Maybe you came because you were feeling down

Maybe you came to relieve some stress.

Maybe you came to wear your favorite suit or dress.

Maybe you came to see an old friend

Maybe you came to meet the next of kin

Maybe you came to show you care.

Maybe you came because the pain you could no longer bear.

Maybe you came to find out why

Someone this sweet had to die

Maybe you came to get one last look at my stone-cold face

Whatever your reasons, don't worry; I'm on my way to a better place.

ONE DAY

One day I'll have no more ties to this earth, and that day, I'll dearly depart.

Hopefully, I'll be able to say I left this earth with a clean heart

I guess that means I'll no longer be living; let's just say I'll be deceased

Please don't try to wake me up. Just let my soul rest in peace

No irons in the fire, no skeletons in the closet, throw them all away

If you choose to remember, that's fine, and for my soul, I hope you pray

Those of you who really cared about me, I know just who you are

Hopefully, I'll be able to look down on you upon the brightest star

I'll be your guardian angel within my arms. All of you, I will embrace

Protecting you from all harm with a big smile upon my face

Whenever you need to talk to me, just look real high to the sky

I can't explain why I left. I'm sorry I can't tell you why

I ask of you, please don't cry for me, please don't shed no tears

You may think I've deserted you, but believe me, I'll always be near.

DEATH

I laugh to keep from crying

Sometimes I think I'm dying

The world to me seems so dark

Life to me has lost its spark

I often ask God, why am I here?

To leave this place, I have no fear

I pray in silence, scared to make a sound

Because death on earth is all around

The mood is scary where the moon is

I guess we'll all be leaving here soon

40 days of fire, 40 days of rain

No one left to ease the pain

I learned a smile is just a frown

Draw a smile on paper and turn it upside down

Soon life will be over. Soon life will end

I think I hear death knocking

Please do come in

P.S. ENOUGH IS ENOUGH

I'm a young black man raised and residing in Compton, California. A city that is famous and known worldwide for all the wrong reasons. A city famous for its negativity, corruption, street gangs, and terrible image. Compton is the "butt" of every comedian's joke when they want to refer to the worse of, the worse. To get a laugh even though they have never stepped foot in the city. So, just when we as citizens thought it was ok to say we are citizens of Compton, bam, we're hit with another rash of unwanted publicity from the media and in the local newspapers. Over the last 20 years, we've dealt with corruption on all levels, from ex-mayors, city council officials, police officers, school board members, both grade school and at the community college, hospital officials, and everything in between. A city famous for being tied to the murders of Tupac Shakur, connections to the Biggie Smalls through ex-Compton resident Suge Knight and the direct killing of well-known rapper, Mausberg and Venus and Serena Williams' sister in a gang shootout. True, all these bad things happened, but enough is enough. Media, give us a break.

We are constantly reading about all the bad leadership at Dr. Martin Luther King Jr. Hospital, which is being labeled as one of the worst of the worst hospitals in the United States. How the state is closing it down, unit by unit. How its funds have been mismanaged out of millions of dollars, how half of the staff is not qualified, it's about to lose its accreditation soon, and the state plans on taking over what's left of the hospital. Last week, Suge Knight was back in the news, or should I say some of his associates who are due to receive life sentences for running one of California's biggest PCP drug operations ever. And the main suspect is still due to be tried for four murders unrelated to the PCP sentence.

Another big story that hit the news last week was the arrest of a Compton Community College board member. He is accused of embezzling the already financially strapped college of, let's just say, a million dollars. Was he not aware of another college board member who was arrested, convicted, and sentenced to jail time for the same thing just a few months ago? Will these elected officials ever learn from all the other ex-con Compton city officials' mistakes? Or should I say misfortunes?

Then there's all the media attention Compton is receiving on the latest rash of gang-related shootings and all the murders. 48 since the first of the year, with only a couple being solved. The media is boasting about how Compton is on pace to break their murder count for last year and how they may break the record the city set in the late 1980s, somewhere around 90 homicides. I just heard on tv, Compton is on pace to regain the title as the murder capital of the United States. Is this really what gang members need to know? Is this really something for them to strive for? The mayor is making big plans to change things he says with programs, gang injunctions, more police, and rewards starting at $500 to turn in people who commit crimes. Does he really think people are going to risk their lives and that of their families for $500 dollars? Compton has 70 police protecting 96,000 people in a city of 10 square miles, infested by drug dealers, street gangs, rapists, robbers, murderers, and people who have total disregard for the law. There is little or lack of jobs or funding from the state to keep our juveniles and young adults off the streets. There are limited resources for education on teen pregnancy and very little being done to address the drug epidemic our city is forced to deal with every day. Seeing the problems firsthand, Compton has nothing to offer other than talk. There's nothing to look forward to for our youth. There aren't any jobs, limited job offers, recreation programs, all parks in the city are "enter at your own risk," there aren't any entertainment venues, movie theaters, dance halls, real job training facilities, skating rinks, amusement parks, you get the picture. Until things change for the better, Compton will continue to get all the negative publicity that we really don't need, and Compton will continue to be the "butt" of all the comedians' jokes when they want to refer to the worse of, the worse when they want to get a laugh. Please, media, enough is enough. Give Compton a break.

A Meeting With My Mind

WARNING!

On May 21, 2009, my foreman at work used the "N" word saying, "It looks like some niggers were having a party on the bus."

On October 13, 2009, another supervisor at my place of employment used the phrase, "Somebody tell that nigger to hurry up."

On November 6, 2009, at the same place of employment, a high-ranking supervisor used the term referring to Blacks on the job as monkeys, saying, "Anybody can teach a monkey how to turn a wrench."

It's hard to believe in 2009, jobs still have people who still, for some reason, just won't let slavery go, which leads to this next poem. And no, I'm not a racist, but this is how I responded to the first incident, not in violence, but I grabbed my pen and pad and began to write, and this is the poem that came out. As I wrote this poem, remember I had no control of my mind or my ink pen, but sometimes you just have to say how you feel.

Parental warning is advised.

A Meeting With My Mind

A NIGGER I'LL ALWAYS BE
(INK PEN RAGE, FORGIVE ME, GOD)

This piece I'm writing is a true story

It occurred on May 21, the year of 2009

You see I was at my place of employment

When I damn near lost my NIGGER mind

My boss used the "N" word on the job today

He said; " look like some "NIGGERS" dirtied the bus"

Usually, I don't use profanity in my poems

But this time I feel it's a must

I thought this Boss was a cool dude, I thought he was O.K

I guess mentally he has yet to make a change

Over the years even I have gained a little common sense

So, to me this boss of mine I now consider strange

I mean where has this man been all these years?

Is a "CAVE" his got damn residence?

Does this white man not know just a couple of years ago

A so called "NIGGER" was voted in as President

A Meeting With My Mind

A so called "NIGGER" holds the highest office in the United States

That makes me more proud of my human race

So next time my so-called boss approaches me

He might just get slapped in his damn face

Throughout the day he approaches me often

Not knowing I heard exactly what he said

So now my whole mindset is different towards him

I now refer to him as "the walking dead"

Luckily, I have pride and dignity for my GOD given race

My so-called boss has just lost all his respect

Let me hear him use the "N" word again

I might place both my hands around his damn neck

Got damn!!! I'm pissed the hell off man

To the highest heights of pisstivity

I just want to take him out to the nearest woods

And let him stare at a noose hanging from a tree

But we're in a recession and I need my job

So, I'll hold my head up high with lots of class

I'm going to be the bigger man because that's how I've been taught

A Meeting With My Mind

And give my so-called boss a damn freedom pass

It's obvious after the progress us so called "NIGGERS" have made
To this white boss of mine, we're still not free
No matter how much he shakes my hand and smiles in my face
A "NIGGER" to this white man I'll always be

ACKNOWLEDGEMENTS

I would like to acknowledge some of the people who have inspired me in some shape, form, or fashion. Helping me stay focused on making my second book possible. First and foremost, I would like to thank God for walking with me every step of the way, my beautiful mother, Edith Hammond R.I.P., my father, Chester L. Hammond Sr. R.I.P., True Faith Baptist Church, my wife, Vicky Hammond, Tyesha, Terrell Jr., Precious, Chesterina, Jasppreresha, April, Jaslyn, Kela, Marvin, Layla, Chester Jr., Vera, Patrick, Cheryl, Waukecha, Tequinta, Marquel, Tavion, Teandre, Paris, Za'Kai, Patrick Jr., Laquan, Anika, Latrell, Becky, Ronald and Mary Jackson, Marvin Criner, Darnell Dixon, Tyrone Crosby, Cap & Drew Pace, Kirk Green, Bernard Johnson, Mandy Carter, Anthony Marquez, Kenny Gee, William Scott, Harold Sweet, Kevin and Bridgett Brokenbough, Kevin Rasco, Wes Zimmerman, Gerald Senior, Dr. Harold Cebrum, Roni's Backstreet Poetry, Suji Ali, all the Front Line Poets, Louise Thomas, Unice Butler R.I.P., Jerry Pardo R.I.P., Maya Angelou R.I.P., Steve Harvey, Ms. Boxie and the A.C.C. Newspaper, Min Valaria Vaultz, Derrick Sesson, Keith Rosary, Arron and Allen House, Mark Williams, Keith Crane, Ruben Encinas, Chris and Vicky Macray, William Burke, Ken Mooney, Chester Jr., Darlene, Kitchen Beav, Melody, Lil P, Parroh, Perris, Zamiah, Jackie Johnson, Ron Airhart, Daniel Gutierez, Jerry Burke, Andre Beavers, Shelia Bush, Martin Rios, Lenora, Tyrone Johnson, Jasmine, Terrell III, Janiyah Crosby, Simone Scott, Edison, T.J, Kim, Mrs. Reed, Aide Castro, Thyra, Pastor Kenny, Bro. Robert Muhammad and the entire family at Mosque #54 of Compton, Pete Guillory, Myra the Firewatch, Arturo Pimemetel, my uncles, aunts, and cousins, and all my other friends whom I did not mention. I love you all the same. The city of Compton for preparing me for any situation, good or bad, that life has to offer. And to all of those who doubted my desire to make my second book come true and my so-called friends who didn't want this project to ever happen, God bless you too. A special thank you to Rhonda Brown aka the Butterfly Bully for helping bring this to life. And on that note, I'm gone again! Terrell Hammond

A Meeting With My Mind

THE HAUNTED HOUSE

A Meeting With My Mind

Made in the USA
Middletown, DE
08 April 2024